Annie Quinn
in America

Annie Quinn in America

Mical Schneider

Carolrhoda Books, Inc. / Minneapolis

Carolrhoda Books, Inc.
A division of Lerner Publishing Group
241 First Avenue North
Minneapolis, MN 55401 U.S.A.

Website address: www.lernerbooks.com

Library of Congress Cataloging-in-Publication Data

Schneider, Mical, 1944–
        Annie Quinn in America / by Mical Schneider.
        p.   cm.
        Summary: To escape the Irish potato famine of the 1840s, twelve-year-old
Annie and her brother emigrate to New York City where they join their older sister
as servants, earning money to bring their family to America, where they discover
that both food and hardship abound.
        ISBN: 1-57505-510-4 (lib. bdg. : alk. paper)
        1. Ireland—History—Famine, 1845–1852—Juvenile fiction.
    [1. Ireland—History—Famine, 1845–1852. 2. Irish Americans—Fiction.
    3. Famines—Ireland—Fiction. 4. Brothers and Sisters—Fiction.
    5. Survival—Fiction. 6. Ireland—Emigration and immigration—Fiction.
    7. Emigration and immigration—Fiction.] I. Title.
PZ7.S3637 An 2001
[Fic]—dc21   00–012650

Manufactured in the United States of America
1 2 3 4 5 6 – SB – 06 05 04 03 02 01

For David, Daniel, and Hannah

1

Annie Quinn wound her way among the crowds at the Ballinrea market letting the fiddle tune sing in her head and her fingers tap a beat on her empty soup pails.

"Don't go looking about," she told herself. "If you look, you'll be hungry."

The toasted scent of oven-made bread wafted out of the baker's shop. A cart rumbled past with crates of squawking chickens. A farmer and his wife, bass and soprano, hawked spring lamb, new cheese, and fresh green onions. Annie's mouth sharpened and watered. She was hungry—ravenously, dizzyingly hungry.

She stumbled forward and collided headfirst with a black frock coat above fine trousers and new boots. A top hat flew into the air and rolled in the dusty road. As if in a dream, Annie reached down and picked it up. She'd never held a beaver top hat. The sleek fur was warm and thick, like a cat basking in the sun.

"Give that to me," a sharp voice cried, and long fingers in a soft leather glove tore the hat from Annie's hand. Without looking, she knew the hat belonged to

Mr. Richard Denby, the rent collector for Lord Cortland.

"I'm sorry, sir," Annie said. In truth, she was only sorry she had to be polite to him.

"Haven't you eyes?" Mr. Denby asked. He inspected the hat closely, brushed it off, and set it back on his head. The brim fit low over his pale forehead, and he raised a glinting single lens to his eye and peered at Annie. He sniffed.

"I know you. You're one of those Quinn brats, ain't you? Your father rents an acre from his lordship, near Cortland Manor, eh?"

"For sure, sir," Annie said, stepping to the side to pass around him. If she lingered, he'd remember that her family hadn't paid the rent. Two years now the potato crop had failed, and two years it had been since the family had seen any real money.

Mr. Denby blocked her way. "Your father's Michael Quinn."

"Was, sir."

"And he has a brother, yes?"

"Had, sir. My father died this winter. Of the hunger, sir. He had a younger brother, Eamon. Eamon Quinn."

"Is the younger brother dead too?"

Annie shook her head. *Was there no pity in the man? Father buried, Bridget in America, the potatoes coming up all rot and stink, and Mam with five children to feed.* She struggled to keep her temper.

"I'm sorry, Mr. Denby," she said, "but I must be going."

"Not yet. Where was your uncle last December, the night of the riot?"

Ah, so that's what you're after, Annie thought. *You want to know who led the men in their ragged coats and with their flickering torches out into the snow and up to the high stone walls of Cortland Manor. Who started the cry to storm his lordship's iron gates and tear open his storehouses? Who slipped away when the British dragoons arrived on horseback to scatter the crowd?*

"Uncle Eamon was passing the evening with us," Annie said flatly. She looked straight at Mr. Denby. "He says it gets lonely in his cabin, by himself and all."

Mr. Denby said, "The devil take you and your uncle." He stabbed the road with his cane and pushed by her. Annie wanted to shout back her own Irish curse but instead waited until he was almost out of range, picked up a stone, and winged it high and fast. Mr. Denby's beaver hat wobbled, and she broke into a run.

❧

At the soup kitchen, an uneven line of villagers was already passing through the cooking shed. Hard as it was to admit to being hungry, it was even more humiliating to shuffle along in a public line. *Like a herd, they were,* Annie thought—*all of them jostled together with their tin cans like cowbells. But these days, the hungry had no choice. No one lived long on pride.*

"Hurry it up. Hurry it up," shouted the guard, and he swung his club at an old woman teetering on the steps.

"Number 230," the clerk bellowed, and Annie hurried into the thick steam. The clerk grabbed her card, punched out the date, and glanced at her ration ticket. "Two full servings, three half," he called to the cook. Annie moved to the soup cauldrons and held up her pails. The cook, his apron soiled and his round face streaked with sweat, poured quickly, and the last drops splashed onto Annie's bare toes. She hopped in pain.

"Move on, move on," the clerk said, and when Annie stood ready to argue, the guard raised his club.

❧

In the west, the sun hung huge and red as if it were pressing close for a last glimpse of the townland's hills and valleys before evening folded them away. Annie lowered her soup pails at the crest of the uneven land and reminded herself that it was glorious, her Ireland. She loved the way the river cradled one field and then another, how the fairy fort with its circle of trees stood alone on the windy ridge. Her family's cabin, the chimney smoke rising over the thatched roof, nestled at the bottom of the hill. Thomas, her younger brother, had come out and was shouting something up to her.

"It's a letter," he called, "from Bridget." He panted his way to the top of the lane.

"Merciful Mother of God," Annie prayed. "I'd almost—"

"She's sent money," Thomas interrupted. "And two tickets."

"Tickets?" Annie felt the breath go out of her.

"They're for us. We're to go to America." Thomas shook the long, blond hair out of his peaked face, and his blue eyes shone.

"But why us?" Annie asked.

"Mam said we're to go to America to live with Bridget and earn money to bring over everyone else."

An old anger rekindled in Annie. Bridget, her beautiful older sister, had left for New York five years ago, before the potato blight and before the hunger. "A bit of adventure," Bridget had said at the time. "Lots of girls are setting out on their own."

But to Annie it was a betrayal. Bridget might be happy with her fine job as a lady's maid in a wealthy home; she might send money and worry about them in her letters, but Annie refused to forgive Bridget for leaving. And now she would make Annie leave as well.

"When?" Annie asked. "When is it we're leaving?"

"Fifteen days now," Thomas said.

"So soon?" Annie asked, her heart sinking.

"Bridget sent money for our food and clothes, and Uncle Eamon will be taking us to Galway and putting us on a big ocean ship."

Annie picked up the soup cans. She wouldn't go, and no one could make her. The sun slipped beyond the horizon and blue shadows lengthened across the road as she headed down the hill.

2

"The neighbors will be coming this evening," Mam said. "It's a last visit they're wanting before you leave." She pressed the jagged nettle leaves into the simmering kettle. On the stool beside the hearth, Annie shredded charlock, the wild mustard plant, into smaller and smaller pieces.

"An American wake is it?" Annie asked. Yellow buds scattered about her lap as if her skirt were a meadow and her hands an angry wind. She'd gone to more than one such leave-taking. The evening started like any other, with friends gathered for storytelling and dancing. But as the hours passed, all the laughing and singing died away until a mother or a father, a husband or a wife, rose to speak. Tonight it would be Mam's turn, and all eyes would turn to her as she drew Annie and Thomas to the center of the room and said her good-byes. Annie shivered and put her hands to her face. They were icy cold.

For days now she had argued with Mam. "Let Uncle Eamon go with Thomas. For sure he can earn more than a twelve-year-old girl can! Or sell the tickets and buy food at the market in Ballinrea—buy seed potatoes to plant this spring. The blight won't be coming a third time."

When Mam ignored her grand ideas, Annie simply announced, "I'll not be going."

Mam put down the long stirring spoon. Her thin hair drifted out of its bun, and she pushed it away impatiently. Before the hunger, Annie remembered, Mam and she had both had thick, shining chestnut hair. "My two Celtic warriors," Father had called them.

"There'll be no more arguing," Mam said. "The neighbors are wanting to say good-bye, and you and Thomas will be here when they come to pay their respects. In the morning, you'll start for Galway."

The kettle bubbled over, and drops of water hissed on the hearthstones. Annie jumped up, and the torn charlock fluttered to the stone floor.

"Say what you want," she cried. "I'll not be going."

☘

Mary McDermott found Annie lying face down on the grass in the center of the fairy fort. "So, Annie," she said, her voice as light as leaves. "I've news."

"Don't want to hear it," Annie mumbled.

"Aye, you do," Mary said. She settled herself, spread a blade under her thumbs, and whistled a low note.

"Never," Annie answered. She was angry and afraid, and the combination made her stubborn.

"Well," Mary said, "I thought you'd want to know, but maybe not."

"Know what?" Annie asked and rolled over.

Mary reached for a purple clover and tied the stem into a ring for her finger. "We're leaving," she said. "Lord Cortland wants his land back, and he'll even pay our passage to Canada to clear us off."

"You're leaving too?" Annie asked. Soon the townland, maybe even all of Ireland, would be empty.

"Aye. All of us."

Annie felt a pang of jealousy. Mary might be leaving, but she would be going with her sisters and her parents. Annie asked, "Where will you go then?"

"To Toronto. To Da's sister, my Aunt Molly."

"And is Toronto near New York?"

"Aye, it is," Mary said. "Very near."

"So we might see each other!" Annie said, happy for the first time in days. She gave Mary a great hug, being careful about her ribcage, where Mary, like everyone else now, had bones as brittle as twigs.

❀

The door to the cabin flew open, and Uncle Eamon ducked his head and entered holding a huge basket with both arms. Over his shoulder, the evening sky was streaked with gold and violet.

"Clear the dresser, ladies!" he cried. "It's a few cakes and a thimble of whiskey, I've found."

Thomas and Roddy and Norah rushed from the hearth to greet their uncle. Annie took the basket and unpacked a dozen eggs, a round of butter, a crock of honey, and a stack of oatcakes.

"And where did you get these?" she asked, holding up three tangled strands of sausage.

Uncle Eamon shook his head and raised his finger. *He's maddening that way,* Annie thought. *Ask him a serious question, and you get a wink or a nod or a bit of a story.*

"Well," Uncle Eamon said, finding a stool and taking the baby, Dominick, on his knee, "It was late at night."

Annie threw up her hands and drew closer.

"And it was cold, and the fire was low, and the chill was creeping into my joints. So, I went to the shed for another lump of turf. And you know my shed," Uncle Eamon said and paused for the children to nod.

In her mind's eye, Annie saw Uncle Eamon's shed. It was filled to the rafters with a jumble of old things—

homemade tables and chairs, painted dressers, spinning wheels, flax combs, and baskets, buckets, and harnesses, mattresses with the straw poking out the seams, and spades, wheelbarrows, and pitchforks. Uncle Eamon, Annie knew, was a tinker. He was a gatherer, a mender, a jack-of-all-trades, and the best uncle anyone could have.

"And from the far corner," Uncle Eamon went on, "from way in the back, came a thread of music."

"The fairies," Norah said, at eight already wise to the ways of the leprechauns. She leaned against Uncle Eamon's shoulder.

"Very gentle-like," Uncle Eamon said, "I moved the chairs and spades, and a long time it took, so many things were piled up one against the other. And I pulled out the old dresser, and what do you think?"

"Tell us!" Roddy cried. He was two years younger than Norah and impatient with almost everything.

"Well. Do ye know?" Uncle Eamon said, looking at each child. "There between the dresser and the wall, perched on the drinking noggin that once belonged to Grandfather Quinn, was a small man in a red jacket and brown trousers. He was wearing a cap and holding a wee fiddle."

"What tune was he playing?" Thomas asked.

"Thomas!" Annie said. He was like that, she reminded herself—always taking people at their word.

Uncle Eamon held his hand up. "The little man didn't say anything. Instead—" he snapped his fingers "—he vanished. And the next evening when I went into the shed, this basket was sitting on the old dresser."

"Will he come again?" Norah asked, twisting a strand of hair around one finger.

"Maybe, maybe not," Uncle Eamon said, and he gently brushed a smudge from her cheek. "But you know how the wee folk are. Just when you think they're gone for good, on a cold, cold night or when the moon is full, there'll be a tune, a bit of a reel coming from behind the dresser or a scuffling in the far, dark corner, and you know they've come back." Uncle Eamon passed Dominick to Norah and stood up. Mam spread an oat-cake with the thinnest layer of golden butter and broke it into pieces for the younger children.

"Thank you, Eamon," she said. "It will be a proper gathering now." Still she did not smile.

Where had Uncle Eamon found the pot of gold, Annie wondered, *to buy all this food?* Whenever Mam sent her to the gombeen man in Ballinrea with something to pawn—Dominick's cradle, Father's old coat—she never came back with more than a penny or two. Stealing was in it somewhere, and she flushed with shame as she realized that Uncle Eamon had come to that.

Voices outside drew Annie out of her thoughts, and,

happy for the distraction, she welcomed in the neighbors. At once skirts swished across the floor, boots clattered on the stones, chatter and laughter filled the cabin. Mam greeted everyone and offered chairs and stools, and Uncle Eamon poured a round of whiskey from the jug he hoisted to his shoulder. Mary McDermott linked her arm through Annie's and drew her into a corner.

"Will you play for us, Annie," Mary asked. "I'll not hear you again so soon."

Annie shook her head and said, "Ask Uncle Eamon. He's grand."

"Eh, Annie," Eamon said, passing by, "you play. My fingers are all stiff." He turned to show his fingers still crooked through the small handle of the whiskey jug.

So Annie went to the shelf and took down the wooden fiddle case. It was dusty with disuse. Father hadn't played for months before he'd fallen sick. The best fiddler in all of County Roscommon—that's how people had spoken of Father. And he'd taught her all his tunes and all the different ways of using the bow and of changing the rhythm and shifting from one key to another. Annie lifted out the fiddle and passed her hand along the neck. The thick strings droned when she plucked them, and the pegs creaked as she tuned. Would Father be listening? She stepped out of the shadows and broke into his favorite, the driving rhythm of "Fiddler's Delight."

"Mrs. Quinn?" Uncle Eamon called to Mam and held out his hand. She gave a smile and a shrug and moved to the center of the cabin. First Mam and Eamon, then a circle of neighbors danced about the tiny cabin. Their shadows bobbed along the cabin walls. An arm crooked above a head, a pair of elbows pointed out, a foot kicked back, a chin turned up. Annie played and played. Only when her arms ached did she draw the bow on one long, last note and lay the fiddle down.

When everyone had found a seat or stood leaning against the wall, Mam said, "It's a sad thing, this taking leave." She drew Annie and Thomas before her. "It breaks my heart, it does."

"Don't," Annie murmured and looked down at Mam's hands with their twisting blue veins and knuckles like pearls.

"Aye, it's a world of troubles we have now, and no end in sight," Mam said as if she hadn't heard. "And my two next oldest off tomorrow."

"Please," Annie said. "Please don't." The time was slipping away so quickly that there were only hours left, and soon it would be morning. She trembled and bit her lip so she wouldn't cry in front of the neighbors.

"Promise me, Annie," Mam said. "Promise me, Thomas. You won't forget your mother. You won't forget your brothers and sister and your uncle. Promise me, you'll not forget your old home. "

"I won't," Annie said, helpless to stop the tears rolling down her cheeks. "I promise. I'll not forget."

"And you'll look after Thomas?" Mam said.

"For sure I'll take care of Thomas." Annie was sobbing deeply now, her chest heaving and swelling, catching and gasping, while behind her rose the wailing of the neighbor women. They were keening now, keening for her and for Thomas, grieving for their loved ones, grieving in high, ancient voices unleashed to mourn the dead.

❦

Later, when the last neighbor had murmured, "The protection of the Blessed Mother on you," and slipped out the door, Annie helped Mam put the younger children to bed and place the two traveling bundles by the door. The one for Thomas had their sheets, the spoons and cooking pot, the noggins, and his clothes. Hers had the biscuits, oatmeal, salt, dried beef, and lemons. Carefully wrapped in paper and tucked under Annie's clothes was the beautiful lace collar Mam had worked for Bridget. The only other thing to go was Annie's new, second-hand pair of boots. The leather sides pinched her feet, and the soles, already coming unstitched, made little flapping noises when she walked. She vowed to wear them as little as possible.

By the last of the firelight, Mam sewed five shillings into the hem of Annie's dress. Annie sat close by on the floor and studied the turf on the hearth. Sometime in the evening, without a word or signal, she had given up the battle to stay at home. When and how it had happened, she couldn't say, but she knew that she couldn't argue any more.

Mam snapped off the thread and announced, "You'll be taking the fiddle."

Annie shook her head. She couldn't.

"Your father would want it."

"You might be needing it." They both knew the fiddle could be pawned to buy food.

"And you might be needing it even more," Mam said. "It's a long way off you're going."

"If I take the fiddle, you'll not have anything of Father's."

"I have your brothers and sister," Mam said. She brought the fiddle case to the door. "Climb into bed."

Annie eased herself next to Norah and drew their quilt around her shoulders. On the hearth, a bit of turf crumbled into embers.

Now the cabin, the townland, and even Ireland began to grow more distant. They faded even as she lay in bed, and a few tiny coals on the hearth sent up a smoky spiral, flared brighter, and died away.

The next thing she knew, the cabin door scraped open, and sunlight streamed across her face.

3

The small, gray donkey Uncle Eamon had borrowed to pull the two-wheeled cart wouldn't be hurried, and Annie was secretly glad. Every squeak of the wheels and groan of the woven rush sides took Thomas and her that much farther from home. After breakfast, Father Flanagan had come to give them his blessing, and Uncle Eamon had tucked the fiddle and the bundles into the cart and handed Thomas up to Annie. Mam held on to the cart's side until the little donkey started walking, and Roddy ran after them as far as the top of the lane, where his legs gave out.

By afternoon, Uncle Eamon had driven them through the village of Ballinrea, across County Roscommon,

and into County Galway. The further he drove, the more the track seemed lined with weedy fields and abandoned cabins. Their thatched roofs had been tumbled in, and their walls jutted out at crazy angles like crooked tombstones. From time to time, a shriveled face stared over a half-door, but mostly the houses seemed empty. In the cloudless blue sky, meadow pipits soared and gave their thin, high call.

"Look, Annie," Thomas said, and he pointed to a family turning the earth in a nearby field. At the sound of voices, the farmer's boy glanced toward the cart, stretched his face in a skull's grimace, and waved the bone that was his arm in greeting. So thin he was, Annie thought. He wouldn't survive until the harvest.

A day later and closer to Galway, a troop of British soldiers cleared the road for a convoy of grain wagons bound for England. Slowly, travelers moved to the sides of the road. Whole families, too weary to go on, collapsed into ditches. No more than piles of rags, they swatted weakly at the wild dogs that sniffed and prowled among them.

Inside the city, the narrow streets and buildings loomed over the donkey cart. In doorways dark as caves, half-naked children huddled on matted straw. When the gray donkey stopped at a crossroads, a mob of beggars surged forward.

"Here we are," an old woman cried and plucked Annie's shawl with fingers sharp as talons. "Not a mouthful of bread. And what will become of us?"

A young mother held up her baby, whose stomach was bloated and whose eyes drifted up in his head. "A trifle, Miss," she pleaded. "Not for me, but for my son."

Behind her, a girl flung open her cloak and thrust out an arm half-covered with oozing, purple wounds. Annie shrank back and drew her shawl over her head not to see more of it. She ached to reach the harbor and to have the ship cast off. She would go anywhere and do anything if only she might keep her family safe from such horrors.

Uncle Eamon turned a corner, and a salt breeze welcomed them to the harbor of Galway Bay. Ahead, a boat with its tall prow and shrouded yardarms loomed over a pier teeming with passengers.

Along the pier, the passengers huddled with their boxes and bundles, dull-eyed and pale. Above them the gulls with their metallic caws circled the boat and dipped down into the floating garbage.

❧

In the morning, the huge ship with its tangle of ropes and masts seemed to wake, pull at its mooring, and rock on the swells. All around them, people were beginning to stir and to talk among themselves. Uncle Eamon helped Annie out of the cart, where they'd spent the night, and picked the last bits of straw from her hair.

"I'll not be keeping you," Uncle Eamon said to Thomas and Annie.

"Wait a bit," Annie said. "There's time." She wasn't ready to go, not yet. Uncle Eamon gave Thomas a bear hug and slapped him on the back.

"Thomas, me man, look after your sister."

Annie threw herself on Uncle Eamon. "It won't be long," she said, her words lost in the rough tweed of his jacket. "We'll be sending tickets. You'll come, won't you?"

"Of course, Annie," Uncle Eamon said. "You're my family. You're all I've got. For sure I'm coming." He held her at arm's length and tipped her chin up with his finger. "Now. Keep an eye on Thomas and write as soon as you get to New York." Eamon handed Annie her bundle and the fiddle. "Go on, now." He gave them a little shove toward the ship and did a bit of a step dance to make them laugh.

4

Somewhere above them, a bell began to toll, and the passengers came to life. They pushed and shoved their way up the gangplank in terror that they might be left behind.

"Stay close," Annie said to Thomas as they made their way up the gangplank onto the ship. The sailors moved roughly through the crowd, pushing stragglers to hurry and hushing talkers until everyone was quiet. Annie motioned for Thomas to look up. On the deck above them, a tall, square man with a face set like a stone had stepped up to the rope railing.

"I am your captain, James Woodward," he said. With one hand behind his back, he scanned the passengers as if they were no more than a cargo of timber—and a not very profitable one at that. Annie recognized the look—she had seen the same mean calculation in Mr. Denby's eyes when he came to collect the rent.

"And this," the Captain continued, "is the sailing ship *Spirit of Liberty,* out of New York. Ship's rules will be followed without exception. There will be no drinking, no spitting tobacco, no smoking or lighting candles below deck. Cooking is permitted at the two ovens on deck and only between noon and three. A gallon of water and rations of biscuits and oatmeal will be handed out daily. First and last, the safety of the ship comes before the comfort of its passengers, so I will hear no complaints." The captain finished, waited for any protests, turned, and departed abruptly. The first mate called the names of all five hundred passengers and then released them to find their berths below.

A stampede of men, women, and children swept down a narrow set of stairs and into a room as large as a barn and just as sour. Caught up in the excitement, Annie and Thomas searched among the two-tiered square platforms lining the wall for an upper bunk. The same people who had been so quiet on the pier were now fully alive to the low-ceilinged, foul-smelling hold that would be their home for the next six weeks. They shouted and cursed, fought each other, and squabbled for places far from the open buckets that would soon serve as latrines.

"Annie," Thomas called. "Over here!" He waved to her from a top berth alongside the ship's wall. Annie pushed her way around a knot of arguing women, handed Thomas her things, and pulled herself up beside him. She wasn't even settled before a young man with a tousled head of red hair and a wide smile popped over the railing.

"William O'Shea," he said and tossed over a carpetbag. He climbed onto the platform, reached down, and drew up a pretty woman with soft black hair and flushed cheeks. "My wife, Ellen."

"*Día dhuit,*" Ellen said.

Annie, who knew a bit of Irish, answered, "Día dhuit. God be with you."

"We're from Galway," William explained.

"We're from County Roscommon, and we're going to New York," Thomas said. "Our sister Bridget sent our tickets."

William told them that Ellen's uncle, a Daniel Hennessy, also lived in New York, and he'd promised to meet them and help them find work. After a few more comments about the crowd and the conditions on board, they ran out of conversation.

It was just as well, for Annie was feeling strange in her stomach. The ship rolled, and Annie jumped from the berth, rushed to the deck, and barely arrived at the ship's railing before she threw up.

❧

At first Annie was sick almost all the time. The dip and pitch of the ship and the smell of unwashed, seasick passengers kept her on deck every balmy day and evening. Sometimes Thomas called her to see a pod of whales surface and blow out plumes of water. Another morning flying fish leapt above the waves and the sunlight flashed on their silvery scales. Beneath a crescent moon and a sky more blue than black, an iceberg glided past, craggy as an ancient Irish castle.

When the sea was calm, Annie brought her fiddle on deck and played for Thomas and Ellen and William. Sometimes William danced, and Ellen said if Thomas and Annie thought William were a fine dancer on ship, they should have seen him at home in Galway. He was a great one.

Annie considered the ship a musical instrument in itself. She tucked herself between cargo boxes on deck and listened for hours. The wind sang in the rigging, hummed through the chains, and snapped the sails. Waves slapped the sides of the boat, and high on the crossbars, the seamen chanted, trimmed, and hauled. If it were just staying on deck, Annie decided, the trip wouldn't be so bad. But fair weather never lasted.

At the first sign of a storm, Captain Woodward ordered everyone belowdecks, and the sailors bolted the hatches so that the passengers rode out the storm in suffocating darkness. Thomas helped Annie pull herself onto their bunk and asked, "Did you bring the oatmeal?"

"Aye," Annie said. She put the pot between them, held the handle, and handed Thomas a spoon. "But it's half-raw again. More fit for horses." The two cooking ovens barely served the needs of so many passengers, and when Annie's turn came round, she was so pressed by those behind her that she became badly flustered, and she often pulled the pot off the fire before the oatmeal was fully cooked.

"It won't be long now," Thomas said, but still they ate sparingly. They made each portion last for several days and shared the lemons, sliver by sliver, with the O'Sheas.

In the dark of the hold, Annie took out her fiddle and held it close for comfort. She couldn't play for all the tossing of the boat, but she could finger the notes and pluck the strings. Sometimes William told stories. Thomas liked the animal stories, especially the one where the fox came into the woodsman's cabin, took up the man's pipe, and sat down for a smoke. The woodsman called for his dogs, but the fox tricked the woodsman, stuck out his tongue, and ran off in a flash.

❧

One evening, three weeks after the storm, Thomas fell ill. Annie touched his cheek, and it was burning with fever. *That's how it had started with Father.*

"Thomas," she said, searching among her things for a drinking noggin, "I'm going for water." Carefully, she crawled to the edge of the bunk and let herself down into the center aisle. Around her, the passengers slept fitfully. Somewhere a man snored, stopped, and snored again. A baby whimpered. In the pool of moonlight from the open hatch, an old woman knelt with her rosary and prayed.

Annie recognized the prayer. "Hail Mary, full of grace, blessed art thou among women and blessed is the fruit of thy womb," Annie recited. Silently, she asked the Blessed Mother to keep Thomas from the fever and to bring them all together again.

On the empty deck, the moon had dipped ordinary

sails, anchors, and coils of rope in silver. Annie stole along the moon's path toward the water barrel. The barrel's lid wasn't locked.

"Thirsty, are ye?" a whiskey-soaked voice asked, and the cook stepped unsteadily out of the shadows. He was a short, thick plug of a man with a long pigtail and a pink scar that wriggled like a worm down the side of his face.

"It's for my brother," Annie said. "Just a drop, that's all."

"Come back in the morning," the cook said. He rested his elbows on the lid. "Water's not for the taking, you know that. Captain says it has to last the journey, so just one gallon a day to a family."

"And how often do we get the full measure?" Annie shot back. "Some days you sailors give us a gallon. Other days it's half or even less. And last week, the line wound halfway around deck. You served full measure to a handful, locked the barrels, and let the rest of us go thirsty."

"True," the cook said. He didn't seem at all upset. "Us sailors are a temperamental lot."

Annie thought of Thomas tossing on the wooden bunk below and remembered her shillings. The cook sold whiskey to the men in steerage, even though the captain had forbidden all drink. "I could pay," she said.

"Oh," the cook said. He smiled and the pink worm twisted on his cheek. "That's an idea."

"A shilling."

The cook folded his arms across his chest and waited.

Annie hesitated. "Two shillings," she offered. "And that's all."

"Very well."

Annie slipped two coins out from the narrow channel of her hem, handed them over, and reached for the dipper.

"Not so quick," said the cook. He took the dipper, lowered it into the barrel, and stirred it about. Annie gritted her teeth. He was deliberately churning up the sediment at the bottom, making the water brackish and foul tasting. The dipper came up, tipped into the noggin, and water barely covered the bottom of the cup.

She burst out, "That's not anything!"

"Neither is two shillings."

"And it's foul! You stirred it up."

The cook said, "Has the fever now, your brother? Serious business, the fever. Can't be too picky about water if he's got fever."

Annie eased the shillings out of her hem, and with each coin the cook ladled out a bit more water. When all but the last shilling was spent, she held up her hand.

"Enough?" the cook asked.

"Yes," Annie said. She was close to tears, but she wouldn't cry, and she wouldn't let him take all her money.

"Good," said the cook. He locked the water barrel.

"Remember, your brother was sick, and I gave you your ration early. Mention the shillings to anyone, and I'll have you hauled before the captain. What will your brother do then, my pretty lass?" He leaned close, his sweaty, whiskey smell making her dizzy, and smacked a wet kiss on her cheek.

Furious, Annie rubbed the back of her hand on her cheek until her face burned. She wanted to fling the water at the cook or throw it overboard. Instead she hurried belowdeck and groped her way back to her bunk. William was wrapping Thomas in Ellen's extra shawls.

"I'm sorry," Annie whispered, both guilty and relieved that William was awake. "It took a long time to get the water."

"Ah, now, it wasn't Thomas woke me," William said. "It was the old lady at her prayers." He tipped his head toward the now empty aisle.

"I've water," Annie said, "but it's not much."

William nodded. "Ellen brought some herbs, so I'll make a potion. It will bring down the fever." While Annie held the noggin, William found the powders, sprinkled them into the water, and raised Thomas so that he could drink. When Thomas had finished half a cup, he lay down again, and soon he was no longer trembling.

Annie leaned against the ship's wall, her shawl drawn close around her. Over and over she saw the gleam of her shillings on the cook's palm. She felt his lips on her cheek and his foul breath in her face. In the morning, he'd be waiting for her. She couldn't think of sleep or of rest. She pulled her knees into her chest and let anger and disgust roll over her.

"In the beginning," William said as if they were sitting before the hearth at home, "even before St. Patrick, a mighty clan of warriors roamed all of Ireland."

"The Fianna," Annie sighed, recognizing one of Father's stories.

"Aye," William said. "And the Fianna had twenty-one houses, and each of these twenty-one houses had twenty-one rooms, and each room had twenty-one fireplaces. Around each fire sat twenty-one Fianna."

Annie noticed that Thomas was asleep, and she motioned to William that he could stop, but the man shook his head and kept going. He was telling the story for the melody of the words, for the pleasure of the old times. "And the leader of all the Fianna," William said, "was a fierce, proud man named Fionn mac Cumhaill." Annie nodded. She had heard of him also.

"And Fionn had a son named Oisín, and Oisín had a son, a boy named Oscar. And all the Fianna were at table when the boy Oscar began to tease the warrior Goll. And Fionn grew impatient and said to Goll, 'Why don't ye wrestle him. Teach him his place.'"

"But Oscar was just a boy," Annie said, "He couldn't wrestle one of the Fianna." She stretched out her legs and flexed her toes.

William said, "That's what Fionn began to think, too, and he hurried down to the grove of trees where the two had gone to wrestle. He didn't want the boy being hurt. But on the way, he met Goll already coming back. 'So,' he said to Goll, 'did ye wrestle?'

"And Goll nodded and Fionn asked, 'And how long could you take his hold?'

"Goll answered, 'As long as it would take to run quick around the house.' And Fionn left Goll, and he hurried to meet Oscar. And he found him in the grove picking fruit from the trees. 'So,' he asked Oscar, 'did ye wrestle with Goll, and how long could you take his hold?'

"'Aye,' Oscar answered. 'Goll's a strong man, but I could take his hold. If I liked, I could have taken it for as long as it would take you to go around the world or until sleep or hunger took me over first.'"

Annie imagined Oscar on Goll's back, his arms around the warrior's neck. She saw Goll flip Oscar to the ground, but the boy was up and grappling the man around the chest. And Goll pushed and strained to knock Oscar over, but the boy's legs were planted like oaks on the ground. And then Oscar pushed Goll backward onto the soft grass. Goll staggered up, holding the side of his head, and limped home.

"And after that," William said, "Goll always gave Oscar a bit of room, but Oscar never used his strength against the great warrior again."

Annie smiled, inched down on the platform beside Thomas, and slept.

❧

In the morning, with Thomas and William still asleep, Ellen motioned to the water pails and pointed to the hatch.

"I'm coming," Annie said.

The cook was already lounging by the water barrel, smoking his pipe, and darting his eyes over the line of waiting men and women. *Don't look afraid,* Annie told herself. *It's fear that'll give you away.*

At her turn, Annie showed the sailor her number and held the pail steady for him to ladle out her gallon. She could feel the cook's eyes run over her face and shawl, trying to decide if she were the girl who had paid four shillings for a cup of water. She blushed with the shame of it.

"That one!" he cried to the sailor and pointed his pipe to Annie. "I gave that girl her ration last night." He reached to stop the dipper. "No more water for her."

The sailor looked blankly at Annie and then at the cook.

"A cup of water was all, and foul and bitter at that," Annie said, her voice rising. "And he wouldn't give it until I paid four shillings. Four shillings for water so thick you'd choke on it." She turned to the women in line behind her. "And Thomas my brother—burning with fever, he was."

The crowd shifted uneasily. Annie swallowed hard and asked, in a voice high and close to breaking, "Blessed Mary, what kind of man would be so cruel to a pair of poor children?"

Without waiting for an answer, she thrust her pail closer, and the sailor hurried to fill it. The cook scowled, took a look at the restless crowd, and stepped away.

Afterward when Annie went for water or for a walk on the deck, William or Ellen came with her. If the cook caught her eye, Annie stared back. Eventually he forgot her, but Annie prayed even harder for a quick end to their journey.

5

"What's he look like, your Uncle Daniel?" Annie asked. The *Spirit of Liberty* had come up the East River that morning, and now dockworkers on the pier lashed her to the mooring posts while Annie and Ellen hung half over the ship's rail and scanned the New York waterfront for Bridget and for Ellen's uncle.

"Ah, he's a big man," Ellen said, "and his face is square and as flat as a pond. Even his nose is flat. He broke it in a fight when he was a boy. And he has great ears—like an elephant's they are. I would pull on them when—" She grabbed Annie's arm. "Look!" On the pier below the ship, a wagon careened to stop and a large man jumped to the ground.

"Uncle Daniel!"

"Ellen!" the man called up. "Día dhuit!"

"Día dhuit," Ellen called back.

"I'll be waiting for you here!"

Ellen shouted down. "It's just a minute I'll be." She waved a temporary good-bye and was off to find William.

Dan Hennessy mopped his broad, red face with his handkerchief, rubbed his horse's neck, and said something in her ear. The horse nuzzled against his pockets, and the cart man pulled out a lump of sugar. The fresh sunflowers twined in the horse's hat danced in the summer air. Ellen's uncle seemed like a nice man, Annie thought. She was glad for the O'Sheas, and she wished even harder that Bridget would wave to her from the bustle below.

This wharf seemed busier and more confusing than the pier in Galway. Delivery wagons raced in front of cabs. Men with wheelbarrows blocked carriages, and horse drawn two-wheeled sleds backed up to loading ramps. In the morning heat, a line of shirtless alongshoremen chanted to the lift and heave of the bales they loaded onto waiting carts. Sheltered under silk parasols, two women, each on a husband's arm, met in surprised reunion, and their eager voices drifted lightly up to Annie. No one, she thought, seemed to notice the sadness of the longshoremen's song.

Thomas wiggled his way to the rail and handed Annie her bundle and the fiddle. "Do you think she'll know us?" he asked for the one hundredth time. His sallow face was even thinner after weeks of fever, and his blue eyes stared more than sparkled.

"For sure she'll know us," Annie said. "It's family we are." The crowd on deck began to shuffle toward the gangplank. She tucked her bundle under her arm and took Thomas by the hand.

"Ow, Annie, you're squeezing," he said and pulled away.

Annie scolded. "Remember what Mam said. I'm to look after you."

"I'm old enough," Thomas muttered. "And Uncle Eamon told me to look after you." But he let Annie hold his hand.

A sailor with a calico scarf around his neck untied the guard rope, and the passengers surged forward, one mind with a thousand sharp elbows, knees, and feet moving down the narrow gangplank to solid ground. On the pier, Annie swayed and wobbled, her knees like water. When they finally steadied, she looked around, and Thomas, Ellen, and William had vanished.

A stranger, a boy half a head taller and a few years older, blocked her way. "*Éirinn go brách*," he shouted. "Ireland forever!"

"Excuse me," Annie said firmly, but the boy held his ground. He hooked his thumbs into his vest pockets and cast an expert glance over her bundle, the fiddle case, and her faded plaid dress.

"County Cork," he said. He dropped his bottle-green eyes to where the toes of her cracked boots turned up from their unstitched soles. "Eh, Galway for sure."

"County Roscommon!" Annie said. Her family might be suffering, but they weren't, at least not yet, the wretched beggars she had seen in Galway. "We've a cow and an acre in lease." Well, they'd had a cow, even if she'd been gone for over a year. They'd have her still, if the hunger hadn't come.

"Ah, perfect royalty, we are!" the boy said with a mock bow. "But even Your Highness can't be sleeping under bridges." He winked knowingly and tipped his stovepipe hat over one eye, revealing the greasy stain where his fingers' constant touch had shined the brim dull green. He spoke faster now, almost in a singsong, "It would be Mrs. Gateley's boardinghouse for you. A lovely woman she is, and it's a fine place. No smoking, no drinking, a hot supper every night at six, soft feather beds, and tea in the morning." With a flourish, he pulled a soiled card out of his vest pocket and thrust it forward. Despite herself, Annie took it and read:

Mrs. Maureen Gateley
Rooms for Rent
251 Pearl Street
Finnbarr O'Halloran, agent

She shook her head, "We'll not be wanting rooms, thank you. Our sister, Bridget, is coming for Thomas and me."

Finnbarr O'Halloran stepped forward, beer and pickled onions on his breath. "And it's Mrs. Gateley's where you should be staying, and while you're out getting work, her's will be a safe place to leave your things." He poked his finger into Annie's bundle and called over her shoulder, "Thomas! This way!"

Annie followed his pointing hand, and the next instant the crook of her arm was empty, and her fingertips tingled. Finnbarr O'Halloran dove into the crowd. Frozen, Annie watched him go. All her clothes and the beautiful lace collar Mam had made for Bridget were in that bundle—and the boy had stolen Father's fiddle.

"Stop," she cried, but the word died away under the whistle of the ferry, the toll of the church bells, the "haw" of the cart drivers starting their teams. Annie plunged after Finnbarr, her boots clattering on the wooden pier. He dodged between two lumber wagons. She pushed her way through a gang of small boys. He swerved around a peddler. She jostled a couple strolling arm in arm. The back of his vest was within reach—the fiddle only inches away.

"Stop!" Annie gasped. With a great lunge, she stretched out her hand and tripped over her flapping soles. Her elbows hit the street and her palms skidded across the cobblestones. Ahead, Finnbarr O'Halloran sprinted into the traffic, zigzagged between the carriages, and disappeared.

Annie sat up in tears. The pale scrape on the heel of her hand became a crosshatch of red, and streaks of rust smeared the crumpled card that Finnbarr had given her. "I'll get my fiddle back," she vowed out loud. "You haven't seen the last of me, Mr. O'Halloran."

"Annie?" a voice called. A young woman, tall and slim in a dark green jacket and long skirt, hurried toward her with Thomas in tow. The hair inside her bonnet had deepened from straw gold to a sun-flecked brown, but the blue eyes and the gap-toothed grin were still the same.

"Bridget!" Annie cried. She pulled herself to her feet and hurled herself into her sister's arms.

6

"And he was Irish, too," Annie said. She tried to explain and still hurry to keep up with Bridget. "Unfair, it was. Him being Irish, talking Irish, pretending he wanted to help, then *stealing*." Just saying the word brought a lump in her throat and made it hard to talk.

"Runners and baggage-smashers," Bridget said, "that's what boys like Finnbarr O'Halloran are. A boarding house hires a runner to go to the waterfront and meet the boats. When a passenger comes down the ramp, confused and lost, the runner pretends to be a

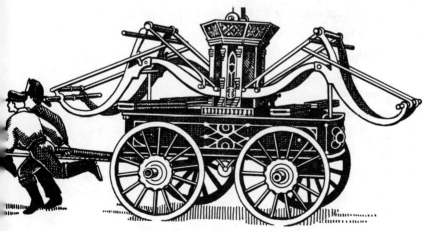

dear old friend or, at least, a helpful countryman."

"But I wasn't lost," Annie protested, "or confused. And none of this would have happened if Thomas hadn't let go of my hand." She glared across Bridget at Thomas.

"I didn't let go," Thomas said. "You loosened up. And I didn't get lost either. I stayed with William and Ellen and their Uncle Daniel. And we had the devil of a time finding *you*."

"Children!" Bridget chided. "It's Independence Day, and if we hurry we can see the procession coming down Broadway." She crossed South Street, ignoring the vendors who called after them.

"Hot corn, hot corn, buy my lily-white hot corn!"

"Clams, fine clams, white as snow. On Rockaway these clams do grow."

"Watermelon, get your fine, ripe wa-ter-mel-on!"

"I'm hungry," Thomas said. Annie wouldn't admit it, but she was hungry too. They'd eaten the last of the oatmeal and biscuits yesterday, and now her stomach was growling.

Bridget stopped suddenly. "Of course," she said, more to herself than to the children. "How could I forget so quickly?" With a coin from her small, fringed purse, she paid for two ears of corn and handed them, still steaming in green husks, to Thomas and Annie.

"This is sweet corn. It comes in white and yellow ears. When it's dried and ground, it's the Indian meal that America's been sending to Ireland."

Annie remembered how, in the first year of the hunger, Father had split stones on the roads to buy Indian meal. She had hated it. It had no taste, it wasn't filling, and if you didn't cook it properly it gave you stomach cramps and the runs.

"Is it safe?" Annie asked, and she looked around to see if anyone on the street was doubled up in pain.

"Of course," Bridget said. "You eat it straight off the cob."

Annie peeled the leaves and silk as if parting the grasses on a nest of small birds. She studied the rows of kernels, as small and white as pearls.

"You're sure now?"

"Go on."

Annie opened wide.

"Wait!" Bridget cried, alarmed and laughing at the same time. "Not like that. An ear of corn is not a carrot. Just eat the kernels." She turned the ear on its side. "Now try."

Annie bit into the kernels, and they exploded with sweetness. Nothing she had ever tasted had been so round on her tongue and crunched with such satisfaction between her teeth. She ate slowly, held out the pocked cob, and asked, "May I have another?"

"Try this first," Bridget said, and she handed Annie a slice of watermelon.

Annie buried her face in the rosy fruit. The sticky juice dribbled off her chin and ran in rivulets down her wrists. She spit the teardrop seeds in the street and slurped at the white and green rind. "Umm," she said and licked the heels of her hands. "More?"

"You'll be sick if you eat too much," Bridget said. "Besides, we need to hurry." She put her hand against Annie's back and urged her and Thomas up Fulton Street.

Annie hadn't gone a block before she slowed to study the banners and signs that hung before the shop windows. But as soon as she puzzled out *grocery, hotel, cobbler,* and *cast-iron stoves,* Bridget had pulled her away again. Only a fleeting glimpse through an open door told her that *saloon* meant food and drink and *taxidermist* meant stuffed birds, stretched animal skins, and a jar full of eyeballs. "For sure, they're glass," Bridget told her.

"Look!" Annie said as they waited for traffic to clear at an intersection. "It's Pearl Street! Can we stop at Mrs. Gateley's?"

"Not today," Bridget said.

"Please?" Annie begged. "It's only a minute I'll need."

"Drums!" Thomas cried and ran toward a muffled tattoo of drumbeats. At the corner of Broadway and

Fulton, he squeezed through the crowd and disappeared. Annie and Bridget pushed in until they found him standing on the curb. Thomas grabbed Annie's hand and pointed.

Down the center of the street, a wide column of men marched smartly behind a raised flag, two pipers, and a drummer. Annie giggled and poked Bridget to look. On their banner, the tailors had stitched a properly dressed Adam and Eve standing below the motto Naked Was I and Ye Clothed Me. Behind the tailors, the cordwainers carried their silk banner of a giant shoe. A wagon rumbled by with printers and apprentices at work on a handpress. As they passed, the men tossed handbills to the waving spectators. The hatters were easy to recognize—their top hats were as black and thick as a flock of crows.

"Who are those gentlemen?" Annie asked. She pointed to an open carriage with elderly men in three-cornered hats, white wigs, and old-fashioned breeches. The crowd cheered even louder.

"They're Patriots," Bridget explained. "They fought in the Revolution seventy years ago and freed America from England."

"Uncle Eamon should be seeing that," Annie said. "He'd like to meet someone who won independence from England. He says he's going to do that for Ireland."

A bell peeled and, as if struck by the clapper, the

columns of marchers split apart and ran pell-mell for the nearest sidewalk. Around the corner, a man with a silver trumpet raced down Broadway.

"Make way! Make way," he shouted. Behind him ran two lines of men in identical red shirts, black pants, and oval-brimmed helmets. Like pairs of fine horses in harness, they pulled a wagon loaded with ladders, long-handled hooks, axes, and leather hoses. In the center of the wagon, a round chimney belched a stream of black smoke.

"What's that?" Thomas shouted, breathless, as all around them more and more bells rang out.

"A fire brigade," Bridget shouted back. "You'll get used to them."

Annie asked, "What's the big black thing?"

"It's the water-pumper. It draws water from underground pipes connected to the reservoir of the Croton Aqueduct. The pumper feeds the water into the hoses, and the firemen spray the flames."

"I want to be a fireman!" Thomas yelled as the men and their pumper turned the corner.

"Yesterday, you were going to be a sailor," Annie said, her ears still ringing.

"No! I'm going to be a fireman."

Annie rolled her eyes, and Bridget gave Annie a look that said, *what are we going to do with him?* Annie felt a great weight lift off her. At least she didn't have to look after Thomas alone.

"Now can we go to Pearl Street?" Annie asked.

"No time," Bridget answered, and she checked a watch pinned to her jacket. "Mrs. Fairchild dresses for dinner at five."

"Well, then, tomorrow?"

Bridget sighed. "Dearest, I'm sorry. If I'd been able to come earlier, none of this would have happened. But Mrs. Fairchild has already been very generous. I can't ask for more time off."

Annie didn't say anything, but she wasn't about to give up. When Bridget hustled them inside a cab, she leaned out the window and craned her neck to see the street signs painted on the buildings.

"Broadway," she said softly. "Broadway Street, Fulton Street, Pearl Street." *Broadway to Fulton to Pearl. Mrs. Maureen Gateley, 251 Pearl Street.*

"What's that building?" Thomas asked and pointed out the window on his side. "The banners. What do they say?"

Bridget leaned over his shoulder. "Barnum's American Museum of Wonders," she read slowly, sounding out each word for him. "Barnum's American Museum. It's a building full of amazing things. You'd never believe what Mr. Barnum has on exhibit." She pointed to another building. "And that's Stewart's

Marble Palace. You can buy anything you might ever want there, and each type of good has its own department." Bridget drew Annie close and touched her hand. "And so. Now you're a great fiddler? You didn't play at all when I was at home."

No, I didn't, Annie thought. But there wasn't a time when she hadn't longed to play, when her heart hadn't lifted to the sharp draw of the bow across the strings. She couldn't explain it, so she joked. "After you left, Father taught me to play so I wouldn't always be wailing after you."

"And can you play 'Kitty Malone?'" Bridget asked, mentioning Uncle Eamon's favorite.

"That one's easy!" Annie said, not realizing Bridget was teasing her. "And 'Araby's Daughter.'"

"The reels too?"

"Yes, and even the double jigs." Annie tucked an imaginary fiddle under her chin and hummed a reel. Thomas whistled the tune and clapped out a counter beat. Bridget scooted forward, lifted her skirts, and battered the cab's wooden floor with the old step pattern.

"You haven't forgotten!" Thomas said, delighted.

"Of course not," Bridget said, her pride offended, and the three of them tapped and whistled and clapped until the cab turned a corner and toppled them together. Bridget pulled the children upright into a hug of silver buttons and lavender scent.

The carriage bounced over the cobblestones. The axles squeaked two loud, one soft, two loud, one soft, and the wheels sang Broadway to Fulton to Pearl. Broadway to Fulton to Pearl.

7

It was the trees that were so distracting, Annie thought. Here was Bridget talking low and serious, and Annie couldn't listen at all. Didn't Bridget notice how the branches reached out to touch above the middle of the street, and how the leaves blocked the sun with their flickering shadows? At home only the fairy fort had trees, and, of course, Lord Cortland had a stand of ancient oaks inside the walls of his estate. But those trees didn't get in the way, and if you stood at the rise on the road from Ballinrea, a whole kingdom of hills and bogs and fields stretched before you. Annie smiled at the memory.

"Annie?" Bridget asked.

"Aye?"

"Are you listening?"

"For sure."

"You are not," Bridget said. "I'll start again. Mr. and Mrs. Fairchild are our employers, and they have three others in service beside myself. Mrs. Cox is the cook, Mr. Belzer is the coachman, and Katherine Akers is the housemaid. They've been Mr. Fairchild's servants for many years, so you must be very polite and follow their instructions."

"I thought you were in charge," Thomas said. "That's what Mam told us."

Bridget shook her head, "Such nonsense! I work for Mrs. Fairchild. She relies on me, but I'm not in charge of anything."

Bridget brushed Thomas's hair out of his eyes, and Annie could tell she was trying to tidy him up. A complete scrubbing, that's what Thomas really needed. His torn, grimy clothes might as well be burnt. Annie knew she wasn't much cleaner. Her oily hair hung about her face, the dirt was permanent now under her broken fingernails, and both of her dresses were stained with weeks of spilling food and wiping her hands.

"Here we are," Bridget said. "Gramercy Park."

The cab pulled up in front of a tall, flat-fronted brick house, and Annie thought she'd never seen anything so grand. A flight of wide marble steps led up to a great door with a gleaming doorknob and brass knocker. On every floor, the windows had glass, even the smallest ones at the top of the house. Bridget had written that she lived on the third floor, so those windows might be in her room, Annie thought.

"Not the front door," Bridget said when Annie and

Thomas stood on the sidewalk, neither one about to move. "Always use the servants' entrance." She opened a low iron gate and led the way down the plain stone steps to a scarred wooden door.

They entered a room as wide as their cabin at home. Where Annie judged the hearth would have been, a huge black stove squatted on four curved legs. All different sizes of kettles and pots boiled on the burners. A few puffed steam, and others rattled their lids. A large woman in a white cap and apron raised a ladle from one of the pots.

"Mrs. Cox," Bridget said. "This is my sister, Annie, and my brother, Thomas. They're finally here!"

Mrs. Cox puckered her lips, blew the steam aside, and sipped the broth. With her eyes squeezed shut, she said, "More salt," and dropped the ladle back into the pot. She stepped forward and let her small black eyes dart over Annie's face, her clothes, her hands, and her unstitched shoes.

"Well, she's certainly none too clean." The cook stepped back and pulled in her chin. "And not nearly as pretty as you, Bridget."

Annie's cheeks burned.

"And the boy," Mrs. Cox continued. She wrinkled her nose and inspected Thomas as if he were a flounder for sale at the fishmonger's stall. "Looks clever enough.

59

Goodness knows, Mr. Belzer is hard pressed for a lad with an ounce of intelligence. Do you like hard work, young man?"

Before Thomas could answer, Bridget said, "Oh, Mrs. Cox, please don't worry. They're wonderful children, and I promise they'll work hard and be a credit to the household."

"Well, Bridget, I'm sure. I'm sure," Mrs. Cox said and fanned the air. "But first, clean them up, clean them up. They smell to heaven."

"You would too," Annie burst out, embarrassed and insulted. "Eight weeks at sea we were! You try staying clean with half a pail of water for cooking, drinking, *and* washing, no privacy for bathing, no sunshine to dry the wash."

"Annie!" Bridget said and grabbed her arm. "Apologize! There's no call to speak like that to Mrs. Cox."

Annie mumbled she was sorry, and Bridget added, "Mrs. Cox, please excuse Annie. She's tired, but that's no call to be disrespectful. You'll see, she means well, it's just that her manners are country ones."

Before Annie could protest that her manners were just fine, it was others' that needed fixing, Bridget hurried her and Thomas into a back room. She closed the door and brought her face close to Annie's.

"Now young miss," she said in a low voice, "you can talk to Mrs. Cox like that once and only once. She'll excuse you this time because of all you've been through, but from here on, while you're in this house, you'll be quiet, polite, and respectful to everyone. Is that clear?"

Annie nodded and fought back her tears.

❧

An hour later, Annie sat in a soft linen nightshirt, jerking a comb through her snarled hair. She had scrubbed herself red in the wide, tin tub behind the wooden screen in the workroom and had dried her hair with one fresh towel after another. Now it was full of knots.

"Can we cut it off?" she begged Bridget.

"Well," Bridget said, lifting the bird's nest from Annie's neck. "I suppose so."

With four snips of the long-bladed sewing scissors, Annie's chestnut hair lay in a heap on the floor. When she shook her head from side to side, the damp ends barely brushed the top of her shoulders. Her head felt light enough to float away from her body.

❧

Bridget led the way up to the attic, opened her bedroom door, and announced, "Here it is then. Your new home."

At once Annie wanted to embrace everything about the little room—the iron bed frame with its plump mattress, bright patchwork quilt, and fat pillows in fresh cases. The three-legged stool was exactly like the ones at home. On the small bureau, the blue pitcher and basin were smooth and cool, and the fringe on the wool shawl folded over the rocker stirred in the breeze. Best of all, the room smelled of lavender.

"Heaven!" Annie said and breathed deeply. She crossed to the little window and leaned out. "And where is Ireland?"

"Beyond the trees and past the church steeple," Bridget said. "I look that way every night."

8

The next morning, while Thomas struggled with his suspenders, Annie tied her plain cotton apron over Bridget's hand-me-down black frock. Her new woolen stockings itched, but when she wiggled her toes in Bridget's old, high-topped shoes, they had plenty of room.

She stood up, tried a few steps, and found that the boots had a mind of their own. They weighed down her feet then strode out ahead—when she stopped, they threw her forward. Regular Fianna boots, they were. Annie lifted her skirts and crossed the tiny room in three great steps. Here was Annie Quinn striding about Ireland, ready to hunt lions and feast at groaning tables.

The door opened, and Bridget appeared in her own black dress with a prim, white collar and a small apron trimmed with a bit of lace. She beamed and said, "Don't you both look splendid now. All proper and ready for service." She plucked critically

63

at the billowing folds of Thomas's shirt.

"Eh, Thomas," she said, "when I bought this shirt in the Bowery, the shopkeeper said that, though it was ready-made, it would fit a boy your age. But look, you're drowning in it." She brushed Thomas's hair so that it stayed flat and out of his eyes. Bridget turned to Annie.

"No one touches a hair on the noble head of a Fianna," Annie said, but she let herself be led to the little mirror that hung above the dresser. Bridget brushed Annie's hair back and tried to trap the strands that curled around her face like tiny flames. She rested her chin on Annie's head so that the mirror showed a stack of faces, the creamy one on top with wide blue eyes and a playful smile. The one below was browned by days on deck, watchful and somber with sea-green eyes framed by long lashes and thick brows.

"Where's that old glorious smile," Bridget said. "The one that Father said was like a reel in itself?"

"Back in Ireland?" Annie asked. *Lost,* she wanted to confess, *in that terrible first year of the hunger.* But she couldn't say that. Bridget was trying so hard to make her feel happy and safe. Instead she said, "Under our bed?"

"Lovely," Bridget said, her eyes dancing. "The old bed, the one against the wall with the high sides and the wooden canopy and the curtain we'd pull across at night."

"The one with the mattress filled with rushes from the river."

"The mattress I said still had a fish in it, a small fish coming for a bit of dinner." Bridget wiggled her hand toward Annie's side.

"And I'd scream," Annie said, squirming away. "And pull the covers over my head. Later, when I was dreaming, I'd roll over and kick you."

"And it was so black and blue I got that I had to come to America," Bridget said with a laugh at the old joke. "Those were great times, Annie." She was quiet for a minute, the brush in her hand, her eyes far away. "Don't worry, love. Things will be better now."

With a certain briskness, Bridget gathered Annie's hair up from her shoulders, separated it into thirds, and plaited it into a short, tight braid that pulled at the corners of her eyes. Bridget twisted the braid into a small bun and anchored it with enough hairpins to make Annie feel like a spiny thistle.

"Ow," Annie said as the hairpins scratched and dug into her scalp. At home, she'd let her hair hang loose so that the wind fanned it out behind her or blew it ahead, a vast auburn flag. Her hair would whip into her face, and she'd push it back from her eyes, peel it away from her mouth. It had been great to have it so free.

"There!" Bridget said when the last hairpin was

wedged in place. "You look proper now. Come along, and I'll introduce you to Mrs. Fairchild." She opened the door, and Annie clung to the banister as she stumbled downstairs, her shoes not completely under her command.

On the first floor, Bridget paused outside a tall double door. "Mrs. Fairchild is lovely, but she likes us to be very proper and very quiet. If she asks you a question, just curtsy and answer, 'Yes, madam,' or 'No, madam.'" She looked gravely at Annie and Thomas. Annie felt a fluttering in her stomach, the old seasickness, and she wanted to ask Bridget to let her go back upstairs, but it was too late.

Bridget had already knocked, and now she was opening the door so that the children could enter a large, sunny room. Mrs. Fairchild rose from a writing table by the window and stood very straight, her hands folded together at her waist. She wasn't at all what Annie expected. She thought Mrs. Fairchild would be old, but she was young and dark-haired with intelligent, brown eyes. Even more surprising, she seemed happy to see them.

Bridget curtsied and said, "Morning, madam. I'd like to introduce my sister, Annie, and my brother, Thomas."

Mrs. Fairchild smiled and said, "Good morning, children. I'm very pleased to have you with us. Your sister is a wonderful help to me, and I couldn't manage without her."

Annie tried a curtsy while Thomas gave a little bow. She was proud of Bridget and forgave her the hairpins. Mrs. Fairchild seated herself and began to describe the household and New York and the responsibilities of being in society, but Annie couldn't listen—there was so much to study.

What grand furniture! And so much of it...just the chairs were a wonder. Some had high backs and padded seats. Others had curved arms and carved legs that ended in little animal feet. The matching tables at either end of the sofa had stone tops the color of fresh cream. The clock above the mantel had a gold-faced sun and a silver moon, and the hearth was spotless, without a trace of soot. Even so, Annie thought, Mrs. Fairchild had far too much furniture. It would take forever to clear the room for dancing, and there'd still be the mirror in its fruit-carved frame to worry about. Bridget tapped Annie's arm—Mrs. Fairchild was talking to her.

"Annie," she said, "you will be our new 'useful girl' and help Katherine with the housekeeping. If you're any-thing like your sister, I'm sure you will be a hard worker and a wonderful addition to our household."

"Yes, madam," Annie said and bobbed a curtsy.

"Now, Thomas," Mrs. Fairchild said. "I understand you like horses."

"Yes, madam," Thomas said, twisting one foot

behind the other. Bridget touched his shoulder for him to keep still.

"You helped your father with the horses back home," Mrs. Fairchild said with an encouraging smile, the kind of smile Annie had seen adults give to children they didn't know very well or who frightened them a bit.

"Yes, Madam," Thomas said. Bridget touched his shoulder again, a sign he should say more. "Helped him every day."

Annie was surprised at Bridget. The closest Thomas had ever come to helping Father with horses was walking the paddocks with him, looking for a winner at the Strokestown races.

"Good!" Mrs. Fairchild said. "Thomas, you will assist Mr. Belzer, our coachman, and he'll fix you a room in the carriage house. Annie will share Bridget's room. Both of you will eat at the servants' table, and each week on Saturday you'll receive your wages from Mrs. Cox. Every ten days or when it's convenient for the household, you'll have half a day free." Mrs. Fairchild nodded to Bridget who curtsied, murmured her thanks, and closed the door behind them.

Outside in the hall, Annie hissed, "Thomas doesn't know the first thing about horses."

"Do too," Thomas said. "And it's more than you know about being 'useful.'"

Bridget gave them a fierce look.

"Hush up, both of you," she warned. "You're bright, able children and if you don't lag about, daydream, or wander off, you'll learn quickly. Remember we have to work together if we want to bring over Mam and the little ones. We can do it. I know we can!"

9

In the music room, Annie watched as a tall, thin girl put her feather duster on the piano and started slowly toward them. She stopped partway, as if sorry that she'd come even that close.

"Katherine," Bridget said, "this is my sister, Annie. She'll be the new useful girl. Annie will be a big help, and now you won't have to do everything yourself."

"Perhaps," Katherine said.

With her long, narrow nose and small, tight mouth, the girl reminded Annie of one of the hedge foxes back home. Her bright, expressionless eyes were already alert to danger. Bridget put her arm around Katherine's shoulders and said to Annie, "Katherine will show you what to do and how it should be done. She's a wonderful housekeeper, and we couldn't manage without her."

"You can start on the front steps," Katherine said, matter-of-fact, and she led Annie down the back stairs

70

and outside to the pump for a bucket of water. Then it was back to the workroom for rags, soap, and a scrub brush, and past Mrs. Cox, who was peeling potatoes and humming. Off-key, Annie noticed.

"Start here," Katherine said, pointing to the top of the marble stairway at the front entrance. "Wash each riser and tread. Check for any scuffs from boots. Scrub the banisters and the railings, and rinse everything twice. Mrs. Fairchild is particular, so we have to do things right. I'll be back to check."

With a sigh, Annie climbed to the top step, dragging up the water pail, sloshing it over her boots. On her knees, she dipped a rag into the water and addressed the marble slab, "Sure, you're already cleaner than any steps I've ever seen." She wrung the water out onto the gray stone and rubbed the rag along the smooth surface. "A lot of cleaning for nothing. Back home, our cabin has no stairs to clean, and even if it had, there'd be no use washing them. Somebody, Uncle Eamon or Roddy or even the chickens would be tracking the dirt right in again. And Mam and I were always sweeping out the dust and the feathers."

Annie dipped the brush into the water, raked the brown soap, and scrubbed the marble so that the soap and the loosened dirt became a cluster of clouds and a line of curving hills.

"Well," she said. "And here's the top of the mountain, and the Fianna are just finishing their hunting." She made a round, soapy sun. "And it's a glorious day, the sky so blue and empty, you might see a sliver of the moon." She soaped a crescent.

A couple of twists from the watery rag and the hills flowed onto the step below. Annie scrambled back, but not before the water soaked the hem of her skirt. She scrubbed the next step down and then the next one, each time telling a bit more of the story. Close to the bottom, her hand hit the bucket, and it clattered to the sidewalk, splattering her fresh apron. Below her, the kitchen door opened and Katherine came up the stairs.

"Still soapy," Katherine said, pointing to a line of foamy scum. "Get fresh water and rinse them again." Before Annie could protest, she was gone.

"Wash the steps yourself!" Annie said to the empty space where Katherine had been. "They never needed cleaning in the first place!"

She folded her arms and sat down on the curb. Even while she fumed, she remembered what Bridget had said about working together. The second time she washed the steps, Annie didn't have the heart to tell herself a story.

☘

The scent of horses came with Martin Belzer to midday

dinner in the servants' dining room. The coachman's face was florid and his side-whiskers bristled as he strained to fasten the buttons of his waistcoat. Thomas followed, disheveled and frowning. Without a glance at anyone, he dropped into the chair beside Annie.

Annie squirmed in her place, uncomfortable to be seated on a chair at a table. Last night and this morning, Bridget had brought their meals up to the attic room and put the tray on the little stool by the window. Annie and Thomas had sat on the floor, the way they sometimes had at home. Now Annie hooked her shoes around the chair rungs and tried to keep still.

"Let us offer thanks," Martin Belzer said. Annie dipped her head, but the blessing was over so quickly that she wondered if the pause while Mr. Belzer cleared his throat hadn't taken longer than the grace itself.

"Mr. Belzer," said Mrs. Cox, "your plate." Martin Belzer passed his plate to Katherine, who passed it to Bridget, who passed it to Mrs. Cox. "Beef stew, Mr. Belzer?"

"Ah! Yes, Mrs. Cox."

"Peas with mint? Fresh this morning!"

"Of course."

Thomas reached across the table and took a potato out of the serving bowl. Even while the steam rose off the papery skin, he broke it open and popped a half into his mouth. His eyes widened in panic, wisps of steam came out of his mouth, and he coughed half-eaten chunks onto his plate. With both hands, he grabbed the pitcher and gulped milk until it dribbled out the corners of his mouth.

"Thomas!" Bridget said. She rushed from her seat, swabbed her napkin against his mouth and chest. "Don't you ever, ever help yourself again. Wait until you're served!"

"But the potatoes were too hot," Annie explained. "They're only just warm at home. You can break them open and not burn your fingers or your tongue."

"Annie!" Bridget spoke so sharply that Annie knew she'd said the wrong thing. At her end of the table, Mrs. Cox raised her eyebrows and pursed her lips. Martin Belzer folded his stubby fingers over the napkin spread across his waistcoat. Katherine sat perfectly still.

"Give me your plate, Thomas," Bridget said and whipped it into the kitchen. Annie tried to ignore the sound food of being scraped into the slops pail. In a minute, Bridget was back and handing the empty plate to Mrs. Cox. With great care, Mrs. Cox gave Thomas a few pieces of stew and carrots, a large serving of peas, and two potatoes. Annie counted four potatoes for Martin Belzer and three for everyone else. That wasn't fair!

Bridget poured Thomas a tumbler of milk and sat down again. Next to her, Katherine cut her meat into perfect brown squares. She speared one with her fork, and chewed it very slowly.

"Well, Bridget," Martin Belzer said as he poured himself a mug of ale. "When are you off to Cincinnati?"

Bridget turned pale. "Oh, Mr. Belzer," she said, "I don't think it's anytime soon. Mrs. Fairchild's new traveling suit isn't ready yet, and there's still her charity work."

Mrs. Cox pressed her napkin daintily to the corner of her mouth.

"Just this morning," she said, as if disclosing an important secret, "she told me, Mrs. Fairchild did, not to plan too far in advance. She's had a letter, you know. Her sister's baby might be early." Mrs. Cox looked around the table, her eye lingering in triumph on Bridget.

Annie stopped chasing peas with her fork and called a cease-fire between her appetite and the infuriating silverware. Was Bridget going somewhere? The very thought broke her hunger. Bridget couldn't leave just when they were finally together.

Thomas pushed back his plate, wiped his mouth on his sleeve, and stood up. "I'm off."

"Use your napkin, Thomas," Bridget said, "and put it away until supper." She pulled her own through the wooden ring next to her plate. "Ask, 'May I be excused?'"

Thomas muttered something, and Bridget nodded.

Annie pulled her own napkin through her ring and rose to follow him.

Bridget asked, "Annie?"

"May I be excused?"

"Yes, of course."

"Wait a minute, missy," Mrs. Cox said. "You'll go directly to the kitchen and start on the pots. Then you'll clear the table and wash the dishes. After that I'll give you the beans to fix for supper, and Katherine will need you in the parlor."

Annie gave a silent appeal across the table, but Bridget raised her coffee cup and drank deeply. *There'd be no help from her,* Annie thought. With a stamp of her square-toed boots, she headed toward the kitchen.

10

From the attic window, Annie watched the orange moon rise above the rooftops. At home she and Mary McDermott used to wonder if this were the kind of moonlight the fairies used when they came to steal a child. "What would it be like," she had asked Mary, "to be stolen away?" Would she be like the girl in the story Uncle Eamon told—the girl who had come back and tapped in the wee hours of the night on her own windowpane?

"Throw an iron hoop over me," she had pleaded to her brother. "Throw an iron hoop, and I'll get home." But though her brother was quick, the fairies were quicker, and they snatched the girl away even while the hoop sang through the air. Still the brother had lived to be an old man, and still he had listened every night at the window, but his sister had never come again. Just the thought of the lonely tapping made Annie ache for Mam.

"Do you ever wonder about home?" Annie asked Bridget, who had come to change into a fresh apron before she served supper to the Fairchilds.

"Of course," Bridget said. "I worry all the time."

"No, I mean, do you ever remember things? Things that happened when you lived at home with us?"

"Sure, now. Lots of things."

"Like what?"

"Oh," Bridget said, settling in the rocker and drawing Annie onto her lap. The chair creaked, and Annie, her head against Bridget's shoulder, let herself be held, just this once, like Dominick or Roddy.

"I remember it was after the harvest," Bridget began. "It was the evening and Mam had put the fire tongs across Norah's cradle to keep the fairies from stealing her away. Thomas was only two, and I was a great thirteen."

"And me?"

"And you, Miss Quinn," Bridget said, talking into Annie's hair, "you were a regular chieftain. Four years old, stubborn and sassy and wanting your way. At night, you kicked and tossed until one night—this night—you rolled out of bed and fell on the floor. And you started wailing. And Norah woke up howling, and Mac . . . "

"Our dog, Mac," Annie interrupted, remembering.

"He was always burying spoons and we were always wondering what happened to them, and he'd be digging them up and bringing them back and dropping them at Mam's feet."

"And Mac was barking," Bridget said. "A perfect uproar, and the door springs open and thumps against the wall, and the moon is so big it fills the doorway. And Father rushes in from the little back bedroom, and he is waving the broom and shouting, 'For sure it's the ghost of me grandfather, Roddy Quinn.'

"And we're all of us up stumbling about and bumping into each other and shouting and moaning. We're all on our knees, saying our prayers and begging Great-grandfather Quinn to forgive us for whatever we've done to upset him. He was a quick-tempered man, and everyone feared him when he was alive. Imagine what he'd do as a ghost!"

"And Thomas?"

"He slept through it all."

Annie thought for a moment. "He still does. He can sleep through anything."

"And so will you," Bridget said. She gave Annie a little push off her lap and toward the bed. Annie slipped under the quilt and caught Bridget's hand before she could leave.

"What did Mrs. Cox mean," Annie asked, "when she said that you'd be off? Are you going away?"

Bridget sat beside Annie. "I had hoped to tell you later, when you and Thomas were more settled," she said. "Mrs. Fairchild is planning to go to Cincinnati, Ohio—that's in the west, you know. Her sister is expecting a baby."

"When?" Annie asked. "When's the baby coming?"

"Ah, now," Bridget said. "At first Mrs. Fairchild thought we'd be leaving in December, but just this afternoon, she told me the baby might be early. November, it seems. Not for months yet."

"But why do *you* have to go? Why not Mr. Fairchild?"

"Mr. Fairchild has business here, and it's Mrs. Fairchild's sister who is having a baby—and so, of course, she wants to help her. Now, a lady can't make her own arrangements. She'll be needing me to see about the hotels, to reserve our places on the coach, and to get our meals."

"But Thomas and me, we just arrived."

"Ah, well," Bridget said. "It's not for me to tell Mrs. Fairchild when she should travel or stay at home."

"You want to go," Annie said. "Don't you?" She rolled over and buried her face in the pillow. "It's the adventure you're wanting, not us."

"Oh, Annie," Bridget said and stroked her hair. "It's not like that. Maybe when I was younger. Maybe before the hunger, when lots of young girls were hoping to try their luck, maybe I did want to strike out and see a bit of the world."

"But we'll never be together if you keep going off."

"So that's what you think, is it?" Bridget asked. "That you'll be alone? Annie, Mrs. Fairchild has promised me a bonus for all the extra work I'll be doing for her. It will put us closer to sending the tickets and that's what we want, isn't it?"

"Yes." Annie's voice was muffled.

"All right, then," Bridget said. "Off to sleep with you."

"Bridget?"

"Aye?"

"When can we go to Pearl Street?"

"Annie Quinn, you don't let go!" Bridget said and sighed. "I'll talk to Mrs. Fairchild."

"Thank you!" Annie said. "It's the best sister you are!"

"It's the most insisting sister you are," Bridget teased back, and she closed the door behind her.

Outside, the night was thick with the conversation of crickets and cicadas. The moonlight floated in the window over the wooden slats of the rocker, across the plaid shawl, and toward the iron bedstead.

"You'll not steal me away," Annie murmured. "Just try it."

11

"Thomas? That you?" Martin Belzer called out from his room in the carriage house. Annie pressed herself into the shadows and held her breath. Mr. Belzer sounded angry. She'd noticed he always seemed angry with Thomas.

"Thomas?" Martin Belzer called again.

A barn swallow dipped beneath the rafters. The

Fairchild's roan horse, Redburn, shook his forelock and sidestepped to the back wall, his jaws working from side to side over wisps of hay. The carriage house fell quiet again, and by the light of a grimy window Annie made her way down the small steps to the cool storage room under the barn.

Thomas lived in a root cellar. Bins for potatoes and turnips stood against the wall. Cobwebs wrapped broken chairs, table legs, and old carriage wheels into gauzy parcels. A pair of deer antlers nailed to the wall served as a clothes rack, and a tattered rug covered the dirt floor. Annie pulled up a one-armed rocker and watched Thomas sleeping on an old straw ticking. He was still thin and sallow. Though they'd been at the Fairchild's for more than a month, Thomas hadn't gained back the weight he'd lost from the hunger and then from the trip over. It was, she knew, because he wasn't eating. Guiltily, she thought back on how she had cleaned her plate at noon and again earlier at breakfast and even at supper the night before, while Thomas only picked at his food.

"Thomas," Annie said gently. "Wake up. You and me, we're going to Pearl Street."

Thomas pulled himself up on one elbow, rubbed his eyes, and asked, "Bridget?"

"We'll have to go without Bridget. Mrs. Fairchild is having another one of her charity meetings."

Thomas swung his feet to the floor, found his shoes and hat, and followed Annie up the stairs. At Redburn's stall, he paused to check the water pail. The horse pricked up his ears, crossed to the stall door, and let Thomas stroke his nose.

Martin Belzer stepped out of his room, his vest flapping open over his rumpled shirt. He said, "What's going on here?"

"It's just me and Annie," Thomas said, his voice still foggy with sleep. "I was checking Redburn's water." Martin Belzer pushed Thomas against a post.

"Don't you talk to me like that!" he said, pressing his palm close to Thomas's throat. "Sniveling Paddy."

"Sir," Thomas said. "Mr. Belzer, if you don't mind—if you're not needing anything—Annie and me will be going out."

"That's better," Martin Belzer said. "Be sure you're back well before supper." He jerked Thomas forward, and he would have stumbled had not Annie caught him.

&

"Why does he act that way?" Thomas asked. They were seated side-by-side on the Broadway omnibus heading to Fulton Street.

Annie shook her head, wondering the same thing. Nothing Thomas did ever seemed to please Martin

Belzer. "We'll have to ask Bridget," she said.

"He never calls me 'Thomas.' It's always 'Pat' or 'Paddy.' When I tell him my name is Thomas, he says all Irishmen are named 'Patrick,' and they're all lazy, reckless spendthrifts. What's a spendthrift?"

"I think it's someone who wastes his money."

"But we're not that way! We're saving our money for tickets."

"Aye," Annie said fiercely. "We're saving every penny."

At the corner of Broadway and Fulton, they climbed down the back steps of the omnibus and headed toward Pearl Street. The street was crowded with afternoon traffic. Two boys rolled hoops in the middle of the street, ignoring the wagon drivers who shouted angrily, waved their arms, and swerved to avoid them. A family of pigs trotted from an alley, snorted at the garbage along the curb, and nosed among the bones and wilted vegetables. The smell of food gone bad, the trickle of sweat down her back, the jostling of so many people with their bundles hurrying off in their own direction made Annie feel small and lost.

Number 251 Pearl Street turned out to be a corner grocery.

"This is it," Annie said to Thomas. Skimpy lace curtains blew from the second-floor windows. "And those must be the rooms."

Thomas pressed his nose to the store window. "Do you think she's here?"

"Says, 'Open,'" Annie admitted, looking at the pasteboard sign hanging in the window. Reluctantly, she turned the doorknob.

Inside, a woman with flyaway raven hair looked up from rubbing the counter with a faded cloth. "Want some bread, do you?" she asked in a voice that was all angles. "Well, I'm all out."

"Ah. Not really," Annie said. She searched for the place to start.

Mrs. Gateley tapped the counter. "Well, what is it?"

"It's the fiddle," Thomas said. "Annie's lost her fiddle."

"Not lost, actually," Annie stumbled to explain. Mrs. Gateley's drumming fingernail muddled her thoughts. "More *taken*. Finnbarr O'Halloran took it—my fiddle—at the dock."

"And when was this?" Mrs. Gateley asked, looking down the long slope of her nose.

"Independence Day," said Annie and tasted defeat. In her mind, the theft was as fresh as yesterday, but really it had been more than a month ago.

"*I* don't know anything about a fiddle," Mrs. Gateley said, advancing on them like a gust of ill wind. "You're here to make trouble. *I* can tell." With her bony arms extended, she swept them out the door, turned the cardboard sign to "Closed," and disappeared into the shadows at the back of the shop.

"Open up, Mrs. Gateley," Annie shouted.

"Open up!" Thomas echoed.

A white arm holding a green pitcher appeared between the lace curtains in the window above them. Annie jumped back as the stream of water hit the stoop.

"Give Annie her fiddle," Thomas ordered the disappearing arm. Behind them, someone laughed.

"Miss Roscommon," Finnbarr O'Halloran said and tipped his greasy hat. "Looking for a room?"

"I've come for my fiddle," Annie said, her temper flaring at the sight of him. "My father's fiddle that you stole."

"Ah. Your fiddle. Of course, you'd be wanting it," Finnbarr said sympathetically. He tucked his thumbs in his vest pockets and turned his attention to Thomas. "And this must be your brother, the one who ran off at the waterfront." His green eyes danced. "Edward, was it? Or James?"

Thomas squinted up at him.

"Thomas," he said. "And I didn't run off. I was waiting for Annie with William and Ellen and their Uncle Dan."

"So, now, Annie," Finnbarr asked as if they were old friends. "How can I help you?"

Before Annie could explain about Mrs. Gateley, Thomas said, "Annie needs the fiddle. It was our father's, and Mam gave it to Annie the night before we left because Annie knows all the tunes."

"Hush," Annie warned her brother. Thomas was entirely too free with what was her private business. "Where is it? Where did you put it?"

Finnbarr O'Halloran pulled his hat over one eye and knit his brows in a way that gave his face a sad and pensive look.

"Faith," he said as if trying to recall a time long past. "I brought your things here, just as I said I would, and I put them in the parlor upstairs for when you would come. But Mrs. Gateley, she has no patience. After a week or so, she gave the bundle to the ragpicker and told me I could take the fiddle up to the pawnshop, to Timothy Dunn at the Golden Globe."

"You pawned it?" Annie cried. By now, the pawnbroker had probably sold the fiddle to someone else.

"Where's the shop?" Thomas asked. "We can go after it."

Finnbarr smiled at him. "Oh, the shop's a small place and hard to find—a bit off Canal on Elm. And the neighborhood's not that safe, it being near the Five Points and all." He glanced at Annie. "If you like, I'll take you."

"And will we go by a firehouse?" Thomas asked, ready to start.

"We could," Finnbarr offered. "Is it a firehouse you'd

like to see, then?"

"Yes!"

"And Barnum's American Museum. Have you been to see that?"

"Not yet," Thomas said.

"Ah. It's a marvelous place," Finnbarr said, warming to his topic. "Last week I saw the Feejee Mermaid."

"What's that?"

"*Who's* that," Finnbarr corrected. "She's a woman, but she can't walk because she's got no legs or feet. Instead she's got a long fish tail."

"Does she have red hair?" Annie asked. She couldn't stop herself. Uncle Eamon had told her that there were red-haired folk who lived under the sea, and that they boiled potatoes and gathered honey just as ordinary souls did on land. He even knew a fisherman who had caught a sea child once in his net, a boy with hair bright as fire. And when the fisherman came home and unwrapped the sea child, the boy scampered under the bed and wouldn't come out for all the cakes and butter in the house. The fisherman poked under the bed with a pitchfork, but still he wouldn't come out.

And so, the fisherman went to the priest who said, "It's his home he's missing. Take the boy in your boat to the spot where you found him and put him back in the sea." Then the fisherman took the child out in his boat, and when he reached the place where he had caught him, the boy dived out of the boat and into the water and was never seen again.

"The Feejee Mermaid!" Thomas said. "Can we go see her?"

"Well, now. I don't see why not. She's on our way. And near a firehouse too." Finnbarr touched Thomas on the arm, and Annie awoke, as if from a spell.

"Leave him alone!" she shouted and grabbed for Thomas. So slick this boy was. Between one word and the next, he could take the very heart out of you. "Come on, Thomas. We'd best be heading home."

"But the fire house and the Feejee Mermaid," Thomas said with a glance at his new friend.

"The Golden Globe, Annie," Finnbarr called. "Canal and Elm. Tell Timothy Dunn I sent you."

"Go to the devil and good riddance, Finnbarr O'Halloran," Annie yelled back.

She didn't have to look to know that Finnbarr had tucked his thumbs in his vest pockets and was grinning at them. The church on the corner struck five on the hour. They'd be late now, and Mrs. Cox would purse her lips, cluck and fuss. Annie and Thomas ran through the crowds, toward Broadway.

12

The late summer and early autumn blurred for Annie into one long household chore. From dawn to evening, Katherine's eagle eyes found things to do—polish the furniture with a mixture of beeswax and turpentine, wash each brick around each fireplace, blacken the hearth with leaded soft-soap.

"Cleanliness is next to godliness," Katherine said when Annie suggested that she'd done enough. So Annie re-dusted the mirrors with a silk cloth and tickled soot out of the carved chair legs with a fine bristle brush.

"Look out!" Katherine said as Annie held the warming pan of coals over the spots on the dining room table. "You're going to burn the table. Here, give it to me. Useless girl, that's what I say."

And Katherine had routines that could not be altered. Once a month, she hauled the feather mattresses to the backyard and heaved them across a thick rope stretched between two posts. While each mattress aired in the September sun, Katherine and Annie unbuttoned the plain cover on the under-mattresses and added new oat straw to plump up the dips and valleys worn by sleeping bodies.

In the evening, when Annie came out to the clothesline, she buried her face in the mattress ticking and pretended she was lying in the sweet, dry grass of the fairy fort. She was telling Mary McDermott a story, and Mary was weaving the grasses into a basket just the right size to hold a fairy baby.

"Daydreaming again," Katherine scolded when she came to help drag the mattresses upstairs and shake them into shape. Annie ignored her sharp tongue and took two corners and gave Katherine two. Together the girls pulled the mattress up the stairs to the proper bedroom and shook the ticking until the feathers fell to the center. Katherine grasped the middle of the mattress and squeezed the feathers back toward the sides. They both leaned over and drummed the feathers until they were evenly spread.

Under Katherine's gaze, Annie tucked on fresh sheets and arranged the pillows in their cases. She drew her hand along the side of each pillow, easing the feathers up toward the center, and then she smoothed over the top and rounded the sides. *Is this the way,* she wondered, *Our Lord made the hills of Ireland?*

On wash day, Annie brought the soiled laundry down to the basement workroom. The household had so many of each different kind of laundry. She sorted everything into piles on the long table and wrote a list of the towels, sheets, napkins, tablecloths, aprons, shirts, shifts, linens, dresses, handkerchiefs, cravats, and pairs of stockings to be washed. Although she was proud of her head for numbers, under Katherine's unbroken gaze Annie often forgot the total number of each item and had to count them again. She cluttered the list with cross-outs and new totals. And smudged the ink when she pressed down the blotting paper.

The list and the laundry went into a basket for the washerwoman's daughter, who came weekly to collect the dirty things and return the clean. The girl was about Annie's height and age, and she always wore white. Her spotless scarf, wrapped high above her head in a series of pleats and folds, gleamed against her coffee-colored skin. She never spoke but watched openly, while Annie, aware of the girl's luminous amber eyes, checked the fresh laundry against her list.

Each week Annie winced at the spelling corrections someone had made on her list. How was she to know that "linnin" was "linen" and "shemeez" was "chemise?" Her pride injured, Annie sulked and suspected the washerwoman's daughter. Secretly, she half-hoped for errors on the girl's part, but she never found any fault in the laundry or in the addition, and so she had to announce the total due.

Then, Mrs. Cox gave Katherine the exact amount of money from the embroidered purse in which she kept the household cash, and Katherine handed the sum to the girl. The washerwoman's daughter wrote "paid in full" across Annie's list and handed it to Katherine. As if it were a treasure map or a love letter, Katherine put the list in her wooden box of household receipts.

❧

"Why does everything have to be so complicated?" Annie asked Bridget, who had come to tuck her into bed. It was late October now, and the air had the snap of a dancer's step. Annie snuggled down and pulled an extra quilt over her shoulders.

"Complicated?" Bridget asked. She stood at the mirror smoothing her hair off her neck. "What's so complicated?"

"Well, taking down all the curtains and putting up new ones."

Bridget smiled. "Oh, that! Katherine's changing the house over from summer to winter. First she'll do the curtains, then the rugs, then . . . "

"Stop!" Annie said. "I don't want to hear it. *We* didn't do that at home, and we were just fine."

"At home *we* didn't have the money for rugs and curtains."

"Well, I'll never have a rug."

"Let's not argue," Bridget said, her voice lighter, almost teasing. "I've something more important." She drew an envelope out of the bureau drawer.

"A letter from Mam!" Annie cried. She sat up and wrapped her arms over the quilt and around her knees.

"August," Bridget began, and settled herself on the bed beside Annie.

"But that was so long ago!"

"Hush," Bridget said and went on. "'Dear Children, we pray for you daily and hope this letter finds you safely together.'"

"But we wrote as soon as we came."

"Annie," Bridget reminded her. "Letters and people can take as long as two months to cross over."

She signalled for no more interruptions and read on:

The harvest is coming in, and again the potatoes are black and foul. Even so, the British have decided to close the soup kitchens. They say we should be able to feed ourselves. But there are no potatoes, and people are draining blood from the cattle and mixing it with a bit of meal to stay alive. Many expect to die as the birds do, with the first frost.

Last week I sold my shawl to buy milk and oats. On the way home, I passed Mr. Denby's house. Bright as noon it was, but his candles were lit, and he stood at his dining table, raising a toast to his guests. Perhaps he felt my eyes upon him, for he came to the window, motioned to his servant girl beside him, and pointed directly at me. It's a basket from the kitchen he'll send out, I thought. Mr. Denby stepped back to his guests. I smiled at the girl, and she closed the curtains.

"Oh, Bridget," Annie said. "How can Mr. Denby be so cruel?"

"There's more," Bridget said. She turned the flimsy paper over and continued:

You remember the Hanleys, who had the spotted dog who never barked. And the Magans—he was the piper, who played for the young people who came to dance at the crossroads. And the McDermotts. Lord Cortland sent them all to Canada. At the last moment, Hugh McDermott couldn't go for the wife took sick, but Mary and her four sisters went on by themselves. Their aunt is to meet them in Montreal and take them on to Toronto. I have given Mary your address and she says she will write to Annie as soon as she is settled.

With all my love,

Mam

"When do you think Mary'll arrive?" Annie asked.

"Oh, now. Let's see." Bridget folded the paper and tucked it back into the envelope. "If she left at the start of summer, by now she'd be in Canada."

"Any day there might be a letter!" Annie thought about the basket on the hall table where Katherine put the Fairchilds' mail. She'd have to tell Katherine she was expecting something from Toronto. She couldn't help feeling just a little important.

"But don't stay up thinking about it," Bridget warned. "It's a while it will take for Mary and her family to get settled. And Mary will have to work, just like you do tomorrow." Bridget cupped her hand around the candle in its pewter saucer and blew it out.

13

Martin Belzer paused, his knife midway to the butter crock. "Thomas, my boy, you're not eating, and we've a long Sunday ahead. The master wants to take Mrs. Fairchild up along the Hudson and show her the autumn colors. Glorious day, you know." Martin Belzer began to fill Thomas's plate. "Eggs, bacon, potatoes, sausage, some of these fine stewed tomatoes, prunes, biscuits, butter, jelly. How's that for a starter?"

Thomas moved back, and Annie's stomach churned. The eggs leaned against the tomatoes, and the prune juice puddled under the muffin.

"Thank you, Mr. Belzer," Thomas muttered, "but I'm not hungry. May I be excused?" He stood up and put his napkin through his ring.

"Oh, no, Thomas. Not this morning," Martin Belzer said, an edge on his good humor. "Poor appetite is not a good sign in a growing boy. Have a seat."

Bridget lowered her fork and studied the air above the platter of sausages. Mrs. Cox ate as she always did, going round her plate clockwise, chewing with little mincing motions, and pausing to sigh before tucking into the next forkful. Katherine stared at Martin Belzer, who pointed his knife at Thomas.

"Eat up, my hearty," he said.

"I won't!" Thomas said, and he ran from the dining room.

"Excuse me," Bridget said to no one in particular. Annie followed her to the carriage house, where Thomas sobbed face down on his bed. Bridget had no sympathy. "Thomas Quinn, what do you think you're doing? You'll come right back, apologize to Mrs. Cox and Mr. Belzer, and eat what you are served."

"Bridget," Annie said, "don't make him. Mr. Belzer will just bully Thomas even more. I've seen him. He twists Thomas's arm and pulls his ear. Mr. Belzer doesn't care whether Thomas eats or—"

"But I do!" Bridget said. She dragged Thomas out of bed and up the stairs. In the yard she stopped to catch her breath and blink in the sunshine. With a sudden tug, Thomas broke free and darted out the back gate.

"Thomas!" Annie cried and started after him.

"Come along, Annie," Bridget said. "We'll apologize for Thomas since he isn't here to do it himself."

❁

"Will you be coming to church with me?" Bridget asked. The dishes were done. Martin Belzer had driven away with the Fairchilds, and Mrs. Cox had taken her thick recipe book and gone to visit another cook.

"May I stay here?" Annie asked.

"He'll be home quicker if you go about your business." Annie shook her head.

"Well," Bridget said, "when he comes back, I intend to talk to him."

In the kitchen, Annie lifted a small wicker basket from the shelf. Thomas would be hungry, but he'd be too stubborn to ask for food. She filled the basket with boiled eggs, potatoes, cheese, bread, a small knife, and a napkin. Later she'd bring him a pitcher of milk.

"What are you doing?" Katherine asked at the doorway.

"Making a basket for Thomas," Annie said. "It's for when he comes back."

"But everything here belongs to Mrs. Cox."

"He didn't eat breakfast," Annie said and stepped around Katherine.

"But you've taken things without asking."

"It's no more than he would have eaten. Besides, what difference does it make when he has his breakfast?"

"The difference," Katherine pointed out dryly, "is that you're taking it away in a basket when no one is looking."

"Thomas works here. He can have his meals whenever he wants."

"Not today, he can't. I'll have to tell her."

Annie wanted to let loose with one of Uncle Eamon's good Irish curses. Something about where Katherine could go and what she could do when she got there and how no self-respecting Irishman need put up with the likes of her. Instead she bit her tongue and headed for the carriage house.

♣

"Annie, wake up." Thomas was shaking her. "I've been everywhere. I walked almost all the way down Broadway. I saw Mr. Barnum's Museum, and it's a big poster of the Feejee Mermaid he's got outside. She's beautiful! And I heard the bells and a fire company came right by me. I didn't have any trouble keeping up. I can run as fast as any fireman."

Annie opened her eyes, and the blue shadows that stretched across the floor made her think of home. The grimy window caught her eye, and she was back in New York.

"It's late," she said. "Where have you been? Bridget and I have worried all day."

"I can take care of myself," Thomas said, and he paced the room with a swagger. "There are lots of boys my age out there. Some even younger. Collecting iron scraps and bottles at the fire they were. One boy said he sells doorknobs and brass trim and makes good money. I could do it, and it'd be a lot better than working for Martin Belzer."

"You can't leave!" Annie said. "We have to stay together."

"Bridget'll be here."

"It's not the same. We all have to work to bring the others over."

Thomas shrugged.

"I'll talk to Bridget," Annie said. Faintly she remembered that she'd promised the same thing once before, but this time she wouldn't forget. "Here, I brought you something." She held out the basket. "Or maybe you're not hungry. Maybe the firemen invited you to Sunday dinner."

Thomas shook his head sheepishly. "Half-famished I am."

"Annie?" It was Mrs. Cox's voice from the yard. In the window the little black boots were moving toward the carriage house.

"You stay here," Annie said. "I'll tell Bridget you're back. But don't go thinking everything is fine. You'll be needing to apologize to Martin Belzer in the morning." She dashed up the stairs to set the table for the Fairchilds' supper.

"But he must try harder," Bridget said. She put out plates and silver for two.

"Why?" Annie asked and passed Bridget the wineglasses. "Mr. Belzer is the one who needs to try harder."

Bridget stopped folding the napkins and said, "Mrs. Fairchild is leaving in a few weeks and, after her stay in Ohio, she is planning to travel down the Mississippi River and meet Mr. Fairchild in New Orleans for the winter season."

"That means," Annie could hardly say the words. "It means the spring before you'd be back."

"It would."

"But it will be only Mrs. Cox to look after us."

"And Katherine."

Annie shook her head. "Not Katherine. She only cares about the cleaning."

"Well," Bridget said, "it's Mrs. Cox who'll look after you. I'll speak to Mrs. Fairchild and ask her to have a word with Martin Belzer. But Thomas will still have to try harder."

14

"Coming to see me off?" Bridget asked Annie and Thomas. She pulled the leather strap through the brass buckle on her new portmanteau and buttoned the coat of her brown traveling suit. Outside the attic window the November wind stripped the last leaves off the trees and tossed them in the street. Thomas kicked the rocker back and forth. Bridget had promised him that things would go better with Martin Belzer. She had talked with Mrs. Fairchild, and now Thomas needed to do his part.

Martin Belzer helped Mrs. Fairchild into the carriage while Bridget shook hands with Mrs. Cox and gave Katherine a real hug. Thomas hung his head and squeezed his fists. With the heel of one shoe, he ground an acorn into the sidewalk.

"Take care of Thomas," Bridget whispered while Annie clung as if to a lifeline. Bridget pried herself free, brushed Thomas's hair out of his eyes a last time, and climbed into the carriage beside Mrs. Fairchild.

Martin Belzer leaned over to Thomas.

"Look sharp, lad," he said. "When I get back, the barn will be cleaned, my rooms swept, and Mr. Fairchild's extra boots shined." He mounted the coachman's seat, and slapped the reins. Thomas headed wordlessly around to the carriage house, while Annie waited and waved good-bye until the carriage had turned the corner.

♣

"Annie, get the fire started in the stove and boil up the water," Mrs. Cox said with a brisk pat to her hand. "You've been a mite sad these last few weeks. Missing Bridget, I dare say? Take my word for it, cooking is the best distraction. While I'm at market, you'll start the veal stock for soup. Be sure to take the scum off when it rises and, in between, polish the good silver. It's on the table."

Annie wondered if Mrs. Cox understood the absurdity of polishing silver that already gleamed. Apparently not, because she was still talking. "Tonight we'll have a little banquet. Mr. Fairchild has asked his business partners over for supper, and I'm to make something from the old days. You know, the time before he was married—the days of my French cuisine."

Mrs. Cox pulled on her winter cape and took up her baskets. "And don't you know," she said with her head tipped to one side, "the next morning after one of my dinners, Mr. Fairchild would come down to the kitchen. He'd stand at the door, bunch up his fingers, and say '*Magnifique.*' That's French, of course." Mrs. Cox puckered up her lips, squinched her eyes closed, and pressed her fingers to her mouth. Her fingers flew out and her black eyes popped open. "Magnifique!" An expression of bliss bloomed on her face, and she almost skipped out the door.

Annie put the veal bones, onions, carrots, and water into a deep stockpot and studied the foam as it rose to the top. At home, the soup from the charity kitchen had no meat and hardly any vegetables. Cabbage-flavored water she'd carried home in her pails. This soup would be filling and delicious, and if only she could get it to Ireland, it would feed her family for a week.

How were Mam and the little ones, she wondered. She counted back the months since she'd seen them. It was December now, so six months it had been. How long since she and Thomas and Bridget had received a letter? Six weeks, in October. And the news in that letter had already been two months old. And the letter that she and Bridget and Thomas had sent in reply would be just arriving. Perhaps Mam would be opening it today and reading about Bridget's plans to go to Ohio. Only Mam wouldn't know that Bridget had already been gone for weeks. The comings and goings of letters, the thought that they might be crossing in midocean, it made her head swim. And the worst of it was that she could never know how her family was managing now, this day, this hour. And that's what she wanted most of all. Annie sank into a chair and forced herself to open the silver chest.

The gleaming knives and serving pieces winked like stars captured in a box of night. *So many different spoons and forks to polish,* she thought. Soup spoons with oval bowls, sugar spoons with narrow bowls, spoons with long handles, spoons with short handles, serving spoons, teaspoons, demitasse spoons. And the forks—broad forks like three-pronged spears for serving the roast, forks for pickles, for fish, and for salad, never mind the forks for dessert. Annie lifted a spoon to her finger and watched it balance.

Mrs. Cox shouldered open the basement door with a basket in each hand and more looped over her arms.

"Well, now, Annie, I see you've not even begun the silver. Never mind. Put the eggs on to boil, bring the block of ice in, and put it in the box. The iceman probably knocked while you were daydreaming. Skim the cream off the top of the milk and whip it for later."

Mrs. Cox tied on her apron and brought out her cookbook. She ruffled through the recipes until she found the one she wanted, brought it close to her face, and inhaled deeply. Each nostril made a little whistling sound as if it were sucking up the printed words.

"Montpellier butter," Mrs. Cox read aloud in a tone that Annie considered reserved for church. "The seasoning of this delicious butter requires knowledge that only practice can provide, for it is necessary to have an exquisite sense of taste to make it perfectly." Mrs. Cox glanced up from the book to check that Annie knew who in the room had the necessary exquisite sense of taste. The cook said, "You'll be making this, but I'll be watching."

Annie curtsied. "Yes, Mrs. Cox."

From that point until the last game hen came out of the oven, Annie never sat down or stopped moving. At six o'clock Mrs. Cox announced, "I'm going to put my feet up. You and Katherine set the table upstairs and find fresh aprons. You may both have a quick bite of cold mutton and a slice of pie from yesterday. Expect to begin serving at seven-thirty."

At the chime of seven, two carriages came round to the front door, and Katherine greeted the gentlemen while Annie took their coats and hats. At seven-thirty, Katherine presented the first bottle of wine to Mr. Fairchild, and at seven-forty, Annie served the consommé. After the soup and the filet of sole in tarragon sauce, Annie cleared the fish plates and opened another bottle of wine. Katherine carved the game hens and served the meat and vegetables on separate platters. Annie marveled at how the gentlemen picked up the right fork without looking.

The conversation barely interested her—something about war with Mexico, the opening of the California territory, and a series of *Tribune* articles about the shells of ancient sea mollusks. But when she served the Montpellier butter, Annie held her breath.

The first gentleman stared bug-eyed at the pistachio-green log and waved it quickly away. Another helped himself almost without a break in his conversation and then forgot to taste it. Mr. Fairchild paused before he cut his portion, seeming to study the tiny flakes of thyme and marjoram within the log. He admired the way the butter rested on its glass dish, which in turn nestled on a mountain of chipped ice inside a glass bowl. Finally, with his monogrammed butter knife, he cut a thin disk and eased it onto the edge of his plate. He let it sit until very carefully he placed a sliver of green butter on a forkful of game hen and ate it. His eyes closed, his brows rose to a peak, and his face swooned in pleasure.

"Magnifique," Annie murmured. Her butter was a success.

Later, after the dishes were done, Mrs. Cox rewarded Annie with a basket of leftovers to share with Thomas. Annie slipped into the carriage house and tiptoed by Martin Belzer's open door, where the heavy smell of pipe tobacco floated over the laughter of the visiting gentlemen's coachmen.

"Look, Thomas," Annie said as she spread a cloth on his wobbly table and unpacked the basket. "Egg custard, onions stuffed with cheese, sautéed mushrooms, chicken drumsticks, and shortbread cookies. Sorry about the strawberry parfait—they ate it all."

Thomas settled himself at the table and picked up an onion so quickly the rings popped out and the cheese spilled on the table. "How are you supposed to eat this?" he asked.

"Very proper," Annie said unfolding her napkin. "With a special fork and a separate knife. And while you're cutting it into tiny pieces, you need to be talking about war in Mexico and President Polk."

Thomas picked up a drumstick and lunged toward Annie. "President Poke?"

"Don't Polk me, Sir!" Annie said.

"Then shall I Polk myself," Thomas said and aimed the drumstick toward his eye.

"Thomas! Gentlemen don't eat that way."

"How, then? How do they eat?" Thomas asked and picked up an egg custard. "Egg custard. Oh, my." He pursed his lips like Mrs. Cox. "Just a bit more, please, if you don't mind."

Annie tried not to giggle. Thomas dabbed the corners of his mouth with the edge of the tablecloth. "Egg custard," he said in a deep voice.

"Egg custard," Annie said in a higher voice.

"Polk the egg custard!" Thomas called out. They laughed so hard that they slumped sideways in their chairs, wrapped their arms around their sides, and begged each other to stop.

"Paddy, come up here," Martin Belzer shouted from the top of the stairs. Thomas sat upright, serious at once.

"He's been drinking," Thomas said in a voice that frightened Annie. She had never heard him sound so flat and hopeless. He tucked his shirt in and ran his hands through his hair. Annie followed him up the stairs.

Martin Belzer stood beside his guests at a table covered with meat pies and tankards of ale. "Gentlemen," he said when Thomas entered, "let me introduce you. This is Paddy Quinn, just off the boat. He can't read, can't write, and can't follow directions. Can you, boy?"

Thomas stepped forward and said, "Sir, if you'll tell me what you want."

"What do I want?" Martin Belzer roared. He picked up his tankard and swung it at arm's length. "What else but more ale?"

The tankard hit Thomas's head, and he yelped in pain. He clutched his ear, and blood spurted between his fingers and ran over his hand.

"Go get it yourself!" Thomas yelled, and he bolted from the carriage house.

In the yard, the gate creaked and swung on its hinges—Thomas had vanished. Annie raced around to the front of the house to find only the gentlemen's waiting carriages. Their horses munched in their feed bags and rang their hooves against the cobblestones. The wind swirled brittle leaves around the lamppost, and the gaslight shone on an empty corner.

15

Toward dawn, Annie drifted off in the rocker, only to wake to the chatter of the sparrows in the bare trees and a thump outside. The paperboy had slung the day's *Tribune* from his bag onto the front steps. *Silly girl,* she scolded herself, *do you think Thomas would be using the front door?*

She crept down the stairs, all the time praying, "Let Thomas be back, Blessed Mother, let Thomas be back," stepped out into the half-light, and crossed to the carriage

house. Inside, the tang of hay was stronger than the winter light. Redburn whinnied low and dipped his head over the stall door.

"You're waiting for him, too, aren't you?" Annie said and stroked the horse's nose. "Stay quiet, now. And remember, it's Thomas who thinks you're the best horse in all of New York City."

A faint light filtered through the cellar window and across Thomas's empty bed. The mismatched chairs stood askew. Cookie crumbs and drumsticks littered the cloth, and an empty egg custard cup wobbled at the edge of the table.

☙

"Where's Thomas?" Martin Belzer said after grace at breakfast. He helped himself to coffee and slathered a scone with butter and honey. "That boy should be up by now. Mr. Fairchild takes the boat for New Orleans this morning."

"Mr. Belzer," Annie said, her voice wavering only a little, "Thomas never came back last night."

Martin Belzer spread grape jam on a second scone, popped it into his mouth, and pushed the crumbs in with his thumb and forefinger. "An accident," he mumbled. "Too close! He knows I'm a big man with a wide reach." As if to demonstrate, he stretched his arm down the table for the corned beef hash.

"Now, we all know Thomas," Mrs. Cox said and patted Annie's arm. "Such an impulsive lad, but he'll be home before evening. You'll see."

"Mrs. Cox," Annie asked, "could I go and look for him?"

"Oh, my dear," Mrs. Cox said, her eyebrows shooting up in distress. "I'm afraid you've just had your afternoon off. Wouldn't do to have another so soon, would it? After all, Mrs. Fairchild has her rules, she does, and even though she's not at home, we have to abide by them." She looked about the table and her eyes stopped at Katherine.

Katherine gave Mrs. Cox a little nod, but a moment later she glanced at Annie with gray, sad eyes—the first hint of sympathy she had ever shown. Annie picked up the coffeepot and took it to the kitchen, half-hoping that Katherine would follow, but she didn't, and when Annie returned, the pot heavy and steaming, Katherine excused herself to start her chores.

Everything about the day was torture. The crisp wind scudded a fleet of clouds across a glorious blue sky. A bonfire in a neighboring yard sent singed leaves and even lighted cinders floating over fences. Each time Annie went to the yard to shake out her feather duster, she cocked her ear and held her breath. Every other hour by the chime of the sun-and-moon parlor clock, she wrapped her shawl over her shoulders and hurried to Fourth Avenue to look for Thomas. She retraced her steps to Third Avenue and lingered as long as she dared.

After supper Annie took her place at the attic window. It was colder now, and the sharp wind bent the flame on her bedside candle, but she left the window open so that she could have a better view of the street. She had promised Mam she'd look after Thomas. And she would. She would sit up again the whole night, watching and listening. She'd search the whole of New York City to find him.

Someone rapped lightly on the bedroom door, and Annie flew to open it. Katherine, still in her black frock, stood in the hallway without a candle. She asked, "May I come in?"

Annie stared in surprise. Katherine slept in a little alcove off the basement workroom and never came up to visit. She disliked talk and called Annie's running comments whenever they worked together, "idle chatter." On her half-day off, she rarely went out but spent her time on some new and (to Annie) unnecessary household project. Still, Katherine had given her a different kind of glance at breakfast, and she must have something to say if she had come up to the attic.

Annie motioned her toward the rocker, pulled over

the little stool, and waited. Katherine rocked for a moment, gave a deep sigh, and said, "I'm so sorry about Thomas. I was hoping this time would be different."

"Different?" Annie asked in surprise and drew her shawl closer.

"Yes. I thought that Bridget would keep Martin Belzer and Mrs. Cox from their old tricks."

Annie stood up, suddenly very cold, and lowered the window. "What kind of tricks?"

"They have a game, a cruel one," Katherine said as if she were beginning a long and familiar story. "It starts in the summer. Martin Belzer insists he needs a boy to help him in the stable, and he really does because he's very lazy. As soon as the boy comes, Martin begins to torment him, calling him names and beating him for small mistakes. By the time Mr. Fairchild leaves in the fall for New Orleans, the boy is ready to run away."

"Just like Thomas," Annie said.

Katherine held up her hand—she wasn't finished—and went on. "Only with Irish boys, it's worse. He hates the Irish. If Mr. Belzer can't make the boy run away, he approaches a policeman, slips him a couple of coins, and says the boy's a thief. The policeman arrests the boy and takes him to the Tombs—that's the city jail—or to the House of Refuge, the children's home on Third Avenue."

"But why?" Annie asked. "Why make the boy run

away or have him arrested? Why not just dismiss him?"

"Because if the lad's dismissed, he can come back and complain to Mr. Fairchild about his poor treatment and even ask for compensation. But once he's been arrested or threatened with arrest, he doesn't dare come round again."

"I still don't understand."

Katherine gave a weary, lopsided smile. "Martin Belzer and Mrs. Cox are Mr. Fairchild's servants. He trusts them and isn't too watchful because they take such good care of him. So when Mr. Fairchild goes away for the winter, he leaves Mrs. Cox with enough money to cover the household expenses and salaries. After Mr. Belzer turns out the stable boy, he and Mrs. Cox take the money meant for the boy. And they spend it on French wines and fancy meals with expensive ingredients.

"In the spring, when Mr. Fairchild returns and asks for the account ledger, for the record of how the money was used, Mr. Belzer says the *boy* stole some of the household funds and ran away not two weeks ago. Mrs. Cox explains how she suspected him of lying and thieving all winter, but she couldn't bear to turn him out into the cold. In truth, of course, he's been gone for months."

"But Martin Belzer wouldn't do this to Thomas."

"Yes, he would," Katherine said. "He's already making plans. Remember the fire around the corner last week?" Annie heard again the bells that had rung in the middle of the night for the fire brigade. "I heard Mr. Belzer tell Mrs. Cox that he was going to tell the police that Thomas set the fire and that he'd seen Thomas run away as the roof blazed up."

"That's wrong!" Annie cried. "What about Mrs. Cox? What would she say if the police came?"

"Oh, dearie," Katherine mimicked Mrs. Cox, "I would never have known, not ever. Thomas seemed like such a sweet child. A bit wild, always running to look at fire brigades, but still."

Annie wanted to laugh at the fluttery, bewildered voice of Mrs. Cox. Here was another side of dull, rule-bound Katherine. She reached out and grabbed Katherine's hands. "Do Mrs. Fairchild and Bridget know about the lying, the stealing?"

Katherine shook her head.

"Mrs. Fairchild hasn't been with us very long," she said. "She married Mr. Fairchild last year and brought Bridget with her. Mrs. Fairchild wants things to run properly, and if she knew, she'd be very upset. Mr. Fairchild stayed home last winter to be in society with his bride. But this year will be like old times."

Katherine reached to the coiled bun at the back of her neck, pulled out the pins, and shook her hair free. The candlelight softened her thin face and caught the strands that fell across her cheeks. "Your sister's been wonderful to me. I've never known anyone so kind."

Annie blushed at the jealousy she'd felt when Bridget hugged Katherine before she left. Looking at the girl as if for the first time, Annie realized she knew nothing about her. "How long have you been here, Katherine?"

"Eight years. I'm sixteen now."

"Eight years! Why stay so long?"

Katherine's eyes lost their flicker of warmth. "Because I'm Mrs. Cox's bound girl."

"What's that?" Annie's voice faltered.

Katherine pulled her hair back, twisted it behind her head, and pushed in the pins. "That means Mrs. Cox came to the Home for the Friendless and asked for a sturdy, obedient girl. The matron who brought me out said I'd lost my father to drink and my mother and sister to fever. Mrs. Cox looked me over as if I were a plucked chicken and the matron said, 'She's on the runty side, but she's trainable.' Mrs. Cox signed the papers, and the matron handed me over. The papers say that Mrs. Cox will provide my keep and give me a religious education. In exchange, I'll work for her until I turn eighteen."

"Katherine, that's horrible," Annie said, sick to her stomach. "It's like Mrs. Cox owns you. How can you stand it? I'd never be a bound girl, not ever."

"Well," Katherine said as she rose to her feet, "make sure you're never an orphan and that Thomas isn't either." She opened the door and listened.

"Thank you for coming," Annie said, and she meant it.

"I'm sorry I didn't tell you earlier," Katherine apologized, "but I didn't think Thomas would leave on his own. I thought I had more time. Still, it's something you need to know."

"I suppose so," Annie said, her mind racing ahead. "For when Thomas comes back."

"And for yourself." Katherine's voice was flat and very quiet. "They'll find a way to get rid of you too. That's what I really came to say." She paused and listened again, but the house was quiet. "Good night." She slipped out the door and disappeared down the stairs.

16

As the days shortened, the long-legged lamplighter with the wide, floppy hat came earlier and earlier to the corner of Gramercy Park. He propped his ladder against the iron pole and climbed the rungs to the globe-shaped glass lantern. At the opening beneath the globe, his flint sparked and the lamp glowed yellow. On the pavement again, he lifted the ladder to his shoulder and walked off into the twilight. The lamplighter made Annie sad—another day had passed, and Thomas was still missing.

To Annie's astonishment, even though the Fairchilds were away, the cleaning continued. On Katherine's orders, Annie pushed the furniture against the wall and rolled up the rugs. Down on their knees, she and Katherine scrubbed the floor not once, but twice.

"Cleanliness is next to godliness," Katherine said again.

"Take Saint Bridget," Annie said as she crawled backwards from the corner, spreading an arc of suds before her. "Saint Bridget was a holy woman, but it wasn't because she was cleaning all the time."

"Is your sister named after her?"

"She is."

"What did she do? Saint Bridget?"

"She was a serving maid, and she knew how to do the milking," Annie said. "And she had her own white cow with red ears, a gift from the pagan priest, the Druid. And she could weave. It was Saint Bridget who wove the first piece of cloth in Ireland. And she could cook."

Annie sat up on her knees. "Once Saint Bridget was cooking bacon for her father and his guests, and an old cur dog scratched at the door. Well, she noticed him, and she opened the door and without a thought to it, she gave the dog her two best pieces of bacon. But then, her father called. And it was time to serve his guests. And Bridget looked to the plate, worried that she wouldn't have enough, but all the bacon was still there." Annie held out the scrub brush as if the bubbles of foam were the strips of bacon. "So there it is."

"What is?" Katherine asked.

"The proof of it," Annie explained. "Saint Bridget still

had all the bacon. Sure, feeding the poor is next to godliness. It's scrubbing the floor, I'd say, that's far behind."

"Well, that may be true in Ireland," Katherine said, "but not in New York." Annie was about to argue, but she stopped. The color rose in Katherine's cheeks, and a light came into her eyes.

Katherine had made a joke. Annie was so startled that she laughed out loud.

❧

Annie marked off the days, then the weeks. Bridget had been gone two weeks, Thomas ten days. Another week passed, and Katherine handed Annie a letter.

"From Ireland!" Annie said and thrust her dust mop behind a curtain. "Don't go." She motioned Katherine to stay. She didn't want to be alone if the news were bad. Annie drew out the familiar thin sheet of paper and read aloud:

October, 1847

Dear Children,

I pray this letter finds you well and thriving under Bridget's care. Annie, you are not to mind about the loss of the collar and the fiddle. I know you are troubled, especially about the fiddle, but the important thing is that all of you are safe and together. Yesterday I sold a bit of lacework, so I have money for milk and porridge and postage.

We are well enough, praise the Blessed Mother, considering all that has happened.

Hugh McDermott heard at last from his sister in Toronto. She was to meet his four girls, so the first of August, the aunt was waiting at the pier in Montreal, but not one of the girls came down the gangplank. A crewman told the aunt that all her nieces died of cholera not but a week out of Liverpool. A thousand others perished on the same boat.

Annie stopped reading, the news so unexpected that it was as if her heart had stopped beating and the only pulse in the room was the tick of the sun-and-moon mantel clock. She had been sure they'd meet again. And Mary had been sure, too. For weeks now, Annie'd glanced at the mail on the hall table waiting for Mary's letter from Toronto. She'd been storing up all the things that had happened to her and Thomas. She'd been turning them over, planning how to say them, and even imagining Mary's laugh when she read the letters. And they'd go on being friends, writing back and forth, and after a while they'd visit. Now Mary was gone. All the things Annie'd been saving welled up inside her like the notes of the saddest ballad.

"Oh, Annie," Katherine said and stepped closer to comfort her. Annie shook her head, determined to finish the letter. She read, "Last week, Mr. Denby came with an order from Lord Cortland. Pay the rent or give up the land."

"Who's Mr. Denby?" Katherine asked.

Annie said, "He's our landlord's agent, the rent collector. Uncle Eamon told us that all over Ireland the landlords are taking back their fields to fence them in for cattle and grain. The landlord's agent asks the poor farmer who has been living on the land for the rent, and when he can't pay, the agent turns him and his family out onto the road."

"Can't the farmers do anything?"

"They're trying," Annie said, and she read on.

Those who could marched in protest to Mr. Denby's house. But he wasn't home, so they hung a scarecrow wearing an old top hat from the tree outside his house. Later that night, someone hid by the side

126

of the road and shot at Mr. Denby as he rode home. The bullet missed, but it's Eamon who has been arrested, though everyone swears that he was drinking at the síbín.

"That's the Eamon who's your uncle?"

Annie nodded. She could barely make herself continue.

Yesterday Mr. Denby came for the extermination, that was the word he used, and he stood in the road shouting, "Hurry it up! Hurry it up!" So I bundled together the clothes and the kettle and what little bedding we had left and brought out the children. The sheriff was there, and he had his men armed, mind you, as if the babies and I were a terrible danger. And one of the men was Peter Reilly, the same Peter Reilly who played whistle to your father's fiddle. He had an axe in his hand and pretended not to know me.

The men went in, chopped the beds and the cupboard apart, and tossed the boards, the creepy stools, the noggins, the fire tongs, the creels, and the little hanging set of shelves for spoons. Like frightened birds they were, all flying out of the cabin into the road.

"Oh, Annie," Katherine cried. "It is so sad."
Annie turned over the paper.

At a signal from Mr. Denby, Peter Reilly and the others went for the roof. They pitched off the thatch and cut through the beams until the timbers groaned and fell inside. Only the walls were still in place, and the men ran at them with a stout log until they caved in, too. When naught was standing but me and the children, the men swung their tools onto their shoulders and left.

The sheriff has padlocked Eamon's cabin. So, with some thatch from our roof and a few boards, we've made ourselves a bit of shelter in the ditch. There's the turf for fire, and we are dry and warm for now. The Blessed Mother only knows what we will do when the snows come.

Pray for us.

Mam

Annie held the letter and looked out the window, only faintly aware that Katherine had left. On the dirt road before the cabin, the stools and shattered beds, the broken chairs and smashed cupboard lay in the dust. The jumbled heap of boards and nails and reed had once been her home. Out of sight, her mother huddled the little ones to her and hummed a lullaby.

17

"Cream, Annie," Martin Belzer said, even though the little pitcher was right in front of him. Annie passed him the cream, knowing that he was needling her just as he had Thomas. She was the only one at home—Mrs. Cox and Katherine had left early to do the shopping.

Martin Belzer punched the middle of his newspaper. "It says here that Ireland is in a frightful state. Potatoes and carrots have been stolen from a certain Mr. Featherstone's castle. Can't be much of a famine, can it now, Annie, if Mr. Featherstone has potatoes and carrots?"

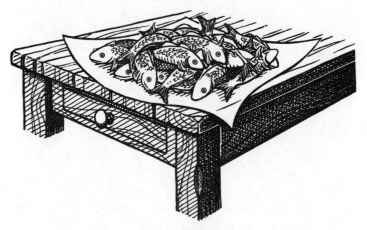

He cracked the top off his soft-boiled egg, dipped a corner of his toast into the yolk, and chewed heavily.

"Ah! Listen," he said and read aloud as if he were the correspondent on the spot. "Irish peasants attack the workhouse at Rathkate. Troops are called, the captain has his ear split apart, and a private loses his eye. See what I mean, Annie. Set up workhouses, and people bite the very hand that feeds them."

Annie tried to keep her voice level. "The workhouse has the food, but the managers won't give it out. They've orders not to feed anyone who has land to farm or a single shirt left to pawn." The ghosts along the road to Galway came back to her, and her voice rose. "When you're not but eyes and bones, when your family has gone to the grave, when you've crawled to the door because you don't want to be dying by the roadside, then you can have food from the workhouse."

"Ah, well," Martin Belzer said pleasantly. He let the newspaper slip to the floor and dropped his egg-stained napkin on top of it. He stood to leave, smoothed down his waistcoat, and smiled at Annie. "I wonder what Mrs. Cox will have for our lunch."

Annie collected the dirty dishes in such a rage that the clatter of knives and plates could have been a battle cry. At the sink, she banged and scoured so loudly that she didn't hear Mrs. Cox and Katherine come back from the market.

"Just a few things to keep my skills up," Mrs. Cox said cheerily. "Wouldn't want to disappoint Mr. Fairchild." She emptied a basket of newspaper-wrapped packets onto the kitchen table. "Fresh fish, Annie. Scale and gut them, while I find a recipe for pheasant."

Mrs. Cox retreated to her sitting room, settled into her rocker, and took up her cookbook. At first she turned the pages with a brisk click, then she slowed to a flick of her finger. All the while, she rocked and made little noises in her throat, a plump dove cooing in her nest.

Annie tumbled out a pile of briny fish. Their scales still glistened, and their clear eyes and translucent fins glinted in the light. Just yesterday, even last night, they had been swimming in the dark waters, rising to the pale green waves, plunging again into the currents. Last summer, while she had tossed afraid and unhappy in the hold of the ship, the fish had been the other travelers, free and at home beyond the ship's wall.

"Daydreaming again, Annie?" Mrs. Cox said, coming back into the kitchen. "Another world is it?"

Yes, Annie wanted to answer, *another world. A world where you could swim away from your troubles.*

"We'll start with the breaded whiting," Mrs. Cox continued. "You already know how to prepare those."

Annie sighed. Breaded whiting was one of Martin Belzer's favorite dishes, and she had seen him eat whole platters of the small fish. Deftly, she gutted the first one, pulled off the skin, twisted the tail into its mouth, and ran a peg through the head to keep the tail fixed in position. She dipped a handful of the circled fish in egg and bread crumbs, fried them, and set them aside.

By noon the kitchen was broiling hot, and Annie had moved on to mock-turtle soup and dozens of tiny meatballs made from a mixture of finely chopped rabbit and veal. The kitchen door opened with a welcome blast of winter air, and the washerwoman's daughter stepped in carrying a basket of clean, folded laundry. When Annie went to call Katherine and Mrs. Cox, the washerwoman's daughter followed her to the workroom.

"Where's your brother?" she asked. "He's never around anymore."

"Thomas?" Annie felt foolish. What other brother would there be?

"Thomas," said the girl. "Where is he? Is he all right?"

Annie didn't know what to say. She was relieved when Katherine and Mrs. Cox came into the workroom.

"Now Annie," Mrs. Cox said, "if you'll pass me the laundry money. I left it right here on the table."

Annie shook her head. "I haven't seen any money."

"Surely you did," Mrs. Cox said. "I put three dollars here before going out to market. Don't you remember?"

"But I was in the kitchen all morning and I didn't see it."

Martin Belzer came in with a bottle of wine and popped out the cork. He said, "Don't think, Annie, that we haven't noticed. Eggs and milk and bread taken without asking. The little paring knife—would I find it in your room or in the cellar?"

Annie clutched the edge of the table. "I never. . . . "

"It's best to be honest," Mrs. Cox said. "Honesty is honesty, no matter where you're from." She glanced at the washerwoman's daughter as if to reassure herself that the same was true in Africa. The girl stood expressionless, her basket snug against her hip.

Mrs. Cox turned to Katherine. "Now tell me, dear. Don't be afraid. Did you see Annie take the money?"

Katherine looked straight at Annie. She said, "When I was getting my cloak to go out with you, I saw Annie slip the money off the table and into her sleeve."

"Katherine!" Annie said, stunned at the outright lie.

Martin Belzer cleared his throat and passed his hand over the buttons of his waistcoat. "Annie, this is an honest, God-fearing house," he said. "And we won't have any lying or stealing. As Mr. Fairchild's appointed representative, I discharge you. Get your things and leave."

"But Mrs. Cox," Annie said. "I'll pay! I'll take the money out of my wages."

Mrs. Cox shook her head, as if wounded on the ear by bad news. "I won't hear of it. Who's to say the money you bring down isn't the very sum I left on the table this morning? And what about next week? Or the week after? We know how you Irish are. We know your kind." Mrs. Cox made a move forward, but Annie fled upstairs.

When she came back to the kitchen with her things—an old shawl of Bridget's, her change of clothing, and the wages she'd been saving for Mam's ticket—Mrs. Cox ignored her. Instead, she watched Katherine check the clean laundry off against Annie's list. Mr. Belzer poured himself a glass of wine.

Annie tried one last time. "I didn't take the money or a knife. The food was what was owed to Thomas. I brought it to him with some breakfast, and I must have forgotten to bring back the knife."

Martin Belzer swirled the wine in his glass and raised a silent toast. He said to Mrs. Cox, "Thomas says he's doing fine on his own."

"You've seen Thomas?" Annie cried. "You've talked to him?"

"Of course. Yesterday morning," Martin Belzer said. "After breakfast. Thomas was leaving the barn and heading toward the house when I stopped him."

"He went to check on Redburn," Annie said quietly. "And it was me he was coming to see next."

"Oh, but I couldn't let him in, could I?" Martin Belzer asked, stepping toward her. "Thomas is a danger. Always running after fire engines, wanting to be a fireman. I wouldn't be surprised if he's even set a fire or two to bring the engines."

"You sent him away?" Annie cried.

"Of course. But he did leave a message."

"A message?" Annie asked, her voice caught like a bone in her throat.

"He said to tell you that you needn't worry. He has work. As an assistant to someone named Finnbarr, at a Mrs. Gateley's."

18

Annie stood clutching her bundle on a sidewalk with wet granite squares only a shade darker than the winter afternoon. Needles of rain stung her hands and face as she hesitated, uncertain. The washerwoman's daughter climbed the stairs from the kitchen, one hand on the iron banister, the other steadying the laundry basket on her head. Dressed in white, the girl looked, Annie thought, like some kind of angel with wings so high that they met behind her head.

"Where are you going?" the washerwoman's daughter asked.

"To Pearl Street," Annie said, hoping that the girl hadn't noticed her backward glance at the cheerful kitchen.

"I'm going to find Thomas." She set off toward Broadway.

"You shouldn't be out," the girl said and fell into step.

Annie bristled. "What about you? You're out."

"It's different."

"And why is that?"

"Because I know where I'm going."

"And I don't?" Annie asked.

"Maybe a little, but not enough."

This girl is infuriating, Annie thought. "So, you're going to help me?"

"I'm trying."

"Thank you, but you needn't bother," Annie said. She couldn't stand such forthrightness. And she would not be told what to do by a girl her own age. She walked faster.

"Well, think about it," the girl said, keeping up. "What if you can't find Thomas?"

They headed down Broadway, and Annie, the rain soaking through her shawl and onto her shoulders, put out her hand to hail an omnibus. But the girl wouldn't be put off.

"Come home with me," she said. "In the morning, my mother and I will help you make a plan."

"No, thank you," Annie said, the words cooler than she'd intended.

The omnibus drew up to the curb, and Annie found

a seat on one of the crowded benches. The carriage smelled of wet wool. Despite herself, she cleared a circle on the foggy window and peered back to the sidewalk.

As if caught in an oval daguerreotype, the washerwoman's daughter paused to find a path between silver puddles. Everything in Annie yearned to join her.

The omnibus rattled on, swaying from side to side. The conductor braced himself while he collected the fares and raised his voice when he called off the downtown stops—Walker, White, Franklin. At Fulton he pulled the leather strap threaded through the coach's roof to the driver's ankle and said to Annie, "This is your stop."

"Broadway to Fulton to Pearl. Broadway to Fulton to Pearl," Annie chanted on her way to Mrs. Gateley's. In the drizzle Pearl Street was almost deserted. A lone workman hurried along, a sodden newspaper held over his head. A cat peered out of a darkened shop doorway and slipped away when Annie came too close. At number 251, a wooden board half-covered the grocery window, and the sign on the door read "Closed," even though inside a young woman swept between the barrels. Annie knocked.

The young woman shook her head and pointed to the sign. Annie knocked again and pressed her hands together as if in prayer. The girl shrugged, propped the broom against the counter, and unlocked the front door.

"We're closed," she said in a familiar accent. "Open again, tomorrow morning at six."

"It's not groceries I'm wanting," Annie said. "It's my brother, Thomas Quinn."

The girl broke into a broad smile that showed her chipped front tooth and motioned Annie inside.

"So, Thomas is your brother, is he? If he knows what's good for him, he won't be coming back."

"But he *was* here?" Annie asked.

"Aye, he and Finnbarr were here yesterday, but they left late last night."

Annie had never seen this girl before, but whether it was her heavy Irish brogue or her smile or her chipped front tooth, Annie felt she could be trusted. "Please, I need to find Thomas. He's run away from where we were working, and now I've been sent away as well. Do you have any notion where he's gone?"

The girl shook her head. "He and Finnbar, they didn't say. Mrs. Gateley, she hardly gave them time for a Hail Mary. A great battle she and Finnbarr had yesterday evening. Everyone could hear it, especially those who left their doors open, and a few of us who stood at the top of the stairs and saw it all." She pointed to the narrow steps behind her.

"Was Thomas in the fight?"

"Not in the fight, but in the corner, watching," the

girl said. "And it was Mrs. Gateley and Finnbarr going at it—Mrs. Gateley saying Finnbarr had stolen her Canton teapot, cups, and saucers, and Finnbarr spitting, for sure, *spitting*, right here on the floor and sneering, 'What would I be doing with fancy Chinese dishes?'

"And Mrs. Gateley yelling, 'You'd be pawning them to gamble and drink at the Five Points.' A thief she called him, and he called her a few names that I wouldn't be saying out loud. And there was scuffling and more shouting. And Finnbarr says, 'Come on, Thomas,' and the door slams."

The girl stopped to catch her breath.

"But where did Thomas and Finnbarr go?" Annie asked.

The girl waved her hand as if it weren't important and took up her story again. "And we was tiptoeing back to our rooms. Real quiet we were, so as not to excite Mrs. Gateley any further, when there was a great crash. We raced down the stairs, and a brick had come through the grocery window. Glass was everywhere. I'm still sweeping up the little glinty pieces. A fortune it's going to cost to get a new pane for the window."

Annie didn't care about the window. "And Thomas?"

"I don't think they'll be back soon. Mrs. Gateley swore she'd have them arrested. And she would, too."

Annie was suddenly exhausted, crushed by the near

miss of it. She wrapped her shawl around her and picked up her bundle. "Are you sure you don't know where they went?" she asked.

"Sorry," the girl said. She closed the door behind Annie and bolted it. Except for the pool of yellow at the base of the gaslights, the street was dark, and the night had turned colder.

It's back at the beginning I am, Annie thought, moving without a plan down Fulton. At the waterfront, the shops were closed, and the warehouses rose somber and shuttered over South Street. The long row of ships rode gently at their narrow berths. The tall masts, furled sails, and looped ropes seemed thick as a forest. Annie walked below the high prows, the bowsprits saluting her, and though she studied each wooden figurehead, not one gazed down on her. Instead they stared unblinking into the distance, as if dreaming of spray-flecked oceans and great whales and the farthest islands rimmed with white sand.

Annie turned off South Street and lost her way in one narrow alley after another. She crept along the cobblestones in the darkness until her foot struck something solid, and her hand patted a cluster of barrels as high as her waist. She inched one cask forward and squeezed herself into the dry space behind it.

For a long time, Annie couldn't sleep but sat among the barrels with her knees drawn up and her arms around her bundle. Much later she woke to a church bell and a watered-ink sky. Something was snuffling and clicking on the other side of the barrels.

She held her bundle tighter and wedged herself back against the wall. With a crash, the barrel tipped over. A huge pig, its bristled snout quivering, fixed its beady eyes on her and showed long, yellow teeth. Annie screamed, leaped up, and raced down the alley, not stopping until she reached South Street again.

19

"Something to pawn?" Timothy Dunn asked. His blotched face with its red and pink patches, metal spectacles, and fringe of white hair poked around the corner from a back room.

The Golden Globe Pawnshop smelled to Annie of old food burned in rusted frying pans. Broken umbrellas rested on used overcoats. Pairs of boots slumped against each other, too worn at the heels and ankles to stand upright. Along the back wall, a dozen clocks squatted side by side, their faces chipped, their hands all pointing to a different time. Each item wore a tag with a spidery number. Everything seemed as Annie felt—separated from a loving, useful life.

"I've come for me fiddle," Annie said.

"Well, let's have the ticket."

Annie shook her head, wishing it could be so easy. "I don't have one. Finnbarr O'Halloran stole my fiddle last summer. He says he pawned it with you."

"O'Halloran, eh?" Timothy Dunn asked and raised a bushy, white eyebrow. "Tall boy, battered black hat.

Stands like this?" He hooked his thumbs into his own vest pockets.

Annie said eagerly, "That's him."

"Haven't seen him for months. Steals fiddles, does he?"

"And my brother. He has my brother with him."

"Brothers, too?" Timothy Dunn pulled an account book from under the counter and flipped the pages. "I'll take fiddles any time, but not brothers. Not much call for brothers." He chuckled at his own joke.

Annie lifted a hand organ off a dusty pile of coverlets. The crank slipped, and the organ gave a little moan.

"When did you say O'Halloran pawned it?" Timothy Dunn asked.

"I don't know. Independence Day? That's when he stole it at the docks."

"Here it is," the pawnbroker said. "Number 178. Handmade violin and case. Pawned July 5, by Finnbarr O'Halloran." He snapped the book closed. "I've got it around somewhere." He headed toward the back of the shop, and when he reappeared with the wooden case, Annie almost leapt to embrace it.

"Aye!" she said. "That's the one." Timothy Dunn opened the lid, and there was the smooth, curved wood, the funny first peg that slipped if you weren't careful with the tuning, the bow with its fraying strands of horsehair. Annie reached to take the fiddle out, but

Timothy Dunn pushed her hand away.

"But it's mine," she said. "Finnbarr stole it."

Timothy Dunn looked around the shop, over the shelves of rippled books, at the bamboo birdcages, and the glass display cases with their heavy pistols, tortoise-shell hair combs, and silver-headed canes. He sighed and said, "What kind of business would I have if I gave back everything that was stolen?"

"But it was!"

"Probably, probably. Still, I gave Finnbarr $3.50. That's American money, no doubloons or shillings. Before you get your fiddle, I get my money."

Annie thought of her wages in the handkerchief pinned to her chemise. It wasn't nearly enough for the fiddle. Besides, she needed something to live on until she found Thomas, and they'd both have to eat until they found work.

"I could give you a dollar," she said, "to hold it for me."

Timothy Dunn shook his head. He closed the case, and the soiled tag with its spidery number gave a little flap against the wood. Annie could tell there'd be no arguing with or persuading of the man. She headed toward the door, and only when her hand was on the knob did she say, "It's a sin to keep something that's not yours."

Before he could answer, she slipped out onto Canal

Street. For sure, she'd had the last word, but Timothy Dunn still had her fiddle.

❧

"Please, sir, please, madam, I'm looking for my brother Thomas. He has fair hair and blue eyes," Annie said. The morning crowd at the Fulton Street landing streamed off the ferry from Brooklyn, the town directly across the river. Most of the men shook their heads, and a few women put a penny in her palm before they hurried on.

The Fulton Street landing was an easy place to ask for Thomas. The ferry came and went across the river several times a day, and there were always delays. Annie wasn't sure exactly when she had started to beg. The first days, she lived on her savings and refused when a gentleman or a pretty lady held out a two-penny piece or a half-dime. Now her money was almost gone, and she took whatever was offered and even asked for coppers. The important thing, she told herself, was to find Thomas, and to do this she had to eat. When she found him, they would figure out what to do next.

Each morning after the ferry, she headed for the Fulton Street market, pushed through the aisles, and watched the floor for a stray apple or carrot. At the baker's stand, she let herself be jostled into a rack of fresh bread. When no one was looking, she slipped a loaf into the frayed basket in which she carried all of her things. She felt sick to be stealing, and it was wrong, but she reminded herself it was for Thomas.

Outside she zigzagged down the sidewalk, hugging first the storefronts, now the curb. At John Street she spotted a half-dime wedged between two cobblestones. A block further, she stooped for a broken bottle.

She was proud of her sharp eyes, and she noticed how roving gangs of boys and girls collected whatever lay unclaimed on the streets. The children pounced on shards of rope, old newspapers, and bottles. They pinched lumps of coal from delivery wagons and wood chips from the shipyards. Anything that could be picked up and stuffed into a burlap bag could be sold to the junk and rag dealers.

"If you want," one of the girls had said to Annie, "you can join us."

Annie thought about it. It would be nice to be with other girls, to have some company. It was lonely to be by herself day after day and especially lonely at night. But she shook her head—if she joined them, she might be distracted by their company and not notice Thomas when she finally passed him. She could manage on her own, but she was grateful to the girls for showing her one way to make money.

At the corner of Maiden Lane and South Street,

Annie ducked into an alley and found her wooden board and homemade broom—a handful of sturdy twigs she had tied with a length of old rope to a broken cane. She had set herself in business a few days ago as housekeeper for this intersection. Now she stepped into the crossing, shoveled the dung from the early morning traffic into the gutter, and swept the cobblestones clear of handbills, gull and pigeon feathers.

"What would you say now, Katherine," Annie asked aloud, "if you could see how clean I keep my crossing?" Annie shook her head over Katherine. Some days she was furious all over again that Katherine had lied about the laundry money, other days she forgave her because Katherine had no other choice—she was Mrs. Cox's bound girl. Annie was hardest on herself. Here she was, out on the street. She stole food and begged for money, and she still hasn't found Thomas. What right did she have to judge Katherine?

A gentleman in a long coat and leather gloves crossed South Street from the waterfront to Maiden Lane.

"Good day, sir," Annie said and held out her hand. The man glanced down at Annie's broom, reluctantly reached in his pocket, and took out a penny. Not long after, three women gave her two pence, and Annie curtsied. A heavy dray laden with bales of cotton lumbered by, and Annie had to sweep up the puffs of raw cotton that caught like clouds on the cobblestones. She didn't mind dashing into the street—all the running kept her warm.

Two girls came to the curb as if to cross. "Yer corner?" asked the taller one, who had washed-out blue eyes and pale hair.

"'Tis," Annie said warily.

"It was our'n. We had it before," the smaller girl said. *The two must be sisters,* Annie thought. They had the same narrow faces, freckled skin, and lank hair. Neither had a shawl or a cloak, and they were so thin it seemed they might blow away with the next gust off the river.

Annie said, "It's my corner."

"You'll have ta leave," the smaller girl said. Her face was as blank as her voice.

"It's not me who needs to be leaving," Annie said, and she stepped forward. The smaller girl didn't move her feet, but shoved out with surprisingly strong arms, and Annie stumbled backwards off the curb. Before she could get her balance, the tall girl kicked her knees out from under her, and Annie collapsed on the cobblestones.

"It's our corner," said the taller girl. "Ain't it, Ruthie?"

Ruthie nodded, picked up Annie's broom, and said, "It's our broom, too." She looked down at Annie. "You'd better get out of the street. Cab's coming."

At the trot of approaching horses, Annie clambered

awkwardly to her feet. Her skirt was muddy and torn, and her breath came fast and short from surprise and anger. She started out after the sisters but thought better of it. Two against one. She'd never get her corner or even her broom back. She found her basket and moved on.

❀

"Do you have anything left?" Annie asked the old woman at a sweet potato stall by the landing. No one boarding the ferry home to Brooklyn had seen Thomas during the day. Heads down against the wind, few had answered her question, and no one lingered to hand her a coin. Just this once, to keep her spirits up, she would treat herself to a hot, comforting supper.

The old woman poked among the coals in her cast-iron kettle. Her layers of shawls, wrinkled face, and bright button eyes reminded Annie of the apple dolls Bridget and she had made at home. Each body was made from rolled and stitched rags, and the head was carved from an apple that shrank into soft golden folds as it aged. The old woman pulled out a leathery potato and a fire-blackened onion.

"Here's the last of them," she said, her teeth gleaming even and white in the dusk.

Annie wrapped the potato and onion in her handkerchief. Roasted potatoes. Mam had made these sometimes

152

at home, and she'd showed Annie how to prick their skins and bury them in the turf coals, then rake them out on the hearth as a snack for the little ones. Annie held out her pennies, but the old woman shook her head.

"I've seen you here about the landing. Over there at the ferry, you are, most mornings. Neighbors we are. And you wouldn't charge a neighbor for a bit of food, would you? Keep the pennies for some bread and ale. You'll have a fine supper."

Neighbors. Annie hadn't thought about neighbors in months—since she had arrived in New York. Up at Gramercy Park, she hardly knew the people who lived on either side of the Fairchilds. At home, her family knew everyone in the townland, and there was nothing Mam or Father, before he died, wouldn't do for a neighbor. And her parents or Uncle Eamon would never think of taking a payment for a favor or even of hearing a word of thanks. "Your neighbor," Father used to say, "is first of all your friend."

"Do you know a runner named Finnbarr O'Halloran?" Annie asked. This woman who considered herself a neighbor might be able to help her. "He used to work for Mrs. Gateley on Pearl Street."

"Green eyes, black vest, top hat?" the woman said. "Ah. A regular baggage-smasher, that one."

"Have you seen a young boy with him?" Annie

asked, eager again. "About this tall," she held her hand up to her chest, "with fair hair and blue eyes?"

The vendor shrugged. "Couldn't tell, dear. Finnbarr's not been around much since the passenger season ended. But I'll ask my husband. He's a cart man and sees more of the waterfront than I do."

Later, in the back lane Annie had begun to think of as home, she rebuilt the little shed where she slept at night. From old wooden boxes and shipping crates she raised three walls against the rough side of a brick warehouse. With a half-dozen broken boards and a piece of oilcloth, she arranged a roof that kept out the worst of the rain and snow. She even had a tiny fireplace in an old earthenware pot. Tucked inside her shelter and wrapped in her shawl, Annie held the shriveled potato close, and the last of its heat warmed her cheek. A barge on the river sounded a deep alert.

"Saint Patrick came to Ireland in a small boat," Annie told herself, "and he knew no one, and no one came out to greet him. And he traveled the land, and everywhere he went, he met the simple people and the Druid priests and the pagan kings." Annie let herself imagine Saint Patrick landing in New York, walking the waterfront, dodging the wagons and carts, approaching the drunken sailors.

She would go up to him. She'd tell him about

Thomas and Martin Belzer and Finnbarr and the two sisters at the crossing. And he would come to see her little shack. He'd share a sweet potato, and after he rested a bit, he'd give her advice. He would tell her how to find Thomas and how to get her fiddle back.

20

"Don't follow me," the boy said, but Annie couldn't help herself. With his blue eyes and shock of fair hair, the boy could have doubled for Thomas. Well, not really, Annie admitted. Thomas's nose tipped up, his ears were rounder, and he was years younger than this fellow. But the boy had Thomas's eager, loose-limbed stride. Just his walk drew her toward him.

"Don't stare at me either."

"I'm not staring at you," Annie said. She deliberately gazed toward the river.

"Then who were you looking at? No one else around."

The street was choked with late afternoon traffic and pedestrians. "I'm looking for my brother, Thomas Quinn," Annie said almost without thinking and added, "and you look like him."

"Well," the boy said, "then you look like my sister, Norah."

"I have a sister named Norah. She's eight."

"My Norah's four."

For a moment, they stood in silence in the center of the sidewalk until two laborers with battered felt hats and picks and shovels on their shoulders glowered at them for blocking the way. Annie moved to one side.

"Is she around?" Annie scanned the street. What would someone look like who looked like her?

The boy said, "She used to come out with me, but she took sick. Now she's up at the shanty town with Margaret Hennessy."

"Hennessy?" The name was familiar, but Annie couldn't think why.

"The sweet potato woman, by the ferry landing," the boy said. "She's a generous woman. She and her husband knew my parents in Galway, and she took us in after they died."

"I know her!" Annie cried, delighted at the unexpected connection. "She gave me the last of her potatoes and onions. She said she'd seen me at the ferry landing, and we were as good as neighbors."

"Aye, that sounds like Margaret."

Annie couldn't think of anything else to say. She thought about how twice now, complete strangers were starting to connect, if not like family, at least like friends. She didn't want to leave and lose something important. "I'm Annie Quinn."

"Jack Mahan."

"Not Thomas."

"No, not Thomas," the boy said. He shook his head and looked genuinely sorry that the names didn't match. He turned to the passing traffic. A horse-drawn wagon drew up to the curb, and the driver threw a bale of newspapers exactly to the boy's feet. Jack tipped his hat, and the driver moved on. Annie knew that she should, too.

"Well, if you see Thomas," Annie said to Jack, "tell him he can come to the Fulton Street ferry slip in the morning."

Jack didn't seem to hear. He cut the twine and quickly folded a paper for a man who waited impatiently, his collar turned up and a cigar clenched in his teeth.

"Good-bye," Annie said, and she pulled her shawl around her, "and I hope Norah is better soon." She lingered, shifted from one foot to the other.

Jack looked up and grinned. "I'll keep an eye out for Thomas," he said. "It will be like searching for meself."

☘

The rest of the day, it didn't matter to Annie that burly storm clouds chased each other across the slate sky or that the brisk wind off the river bit her ears. In the evening, she wasn't so disappointed when she saw that the sweet potato lady wasn't there. Why, of course,

Margaret Hennessy was uptown caring for Norah Mahan, who had Annie's own chestnut brown hair and sea-green eyes.

Annie waited at the landing, but no one going on or off the Brooklyn ferry had seen Thomas. For once, it didn't matter so much. Margaret Hennessy had promised to look for Finnbarr and Jack Mahan would watch for Thomas. She wasn't so alone now.

She rummaged in the refuse bin, pulled out a tattered copy of the day's paper, and saw that the date was December 31. The front page had an installment of a novel by Charles Dickens, *Domby and Son*. She'd save that for later. The ads were all for New Year's Day presents—toys and music boxes, cakes and sweets—all the things she'd seen in the shop windows. Buried on the inside pages was the news from Ireland.

"Starvation in the midst of plenty," she read and shivered to think of Mam and the babies. Tomorrow, it would be 1848. Would this be the year that they would all be together again?

"Blessed Mother, bring us all together," she prayed.

The bells rang out at midnight and a sharp crack split the air. Annie sat straight up, fully awake. Another pistol shot, and then another. Annie held her breath.

The acrid smell of gunpowder drifted closer on the dank air. Footsteps echoed in the alley. Who was coming?

Was he looking for her? Where could she hide? She moved to a corner of her shed and stared into the darkness, straining to hear his footsteps. Her palms sweated and her head pounded. Several men shouted, but it was hard to understand them. Then it was quiet.

A hoarse voice called, "Hap-py New Year," and a pistol cracked again. Annie dissolved, crying and shivering with fear and relief. A strange country it was, where men used guns to celebrate a holiday. At the end of the alley, a man laughed. Someone called out and another answered. The footsteps faded, the gunshots echoed from further down South Street.

On New Year's Day, Annie woke late and listened for more blasts. She crept down the alley and peered around the corner.

The street was empty.

The taverns were closed, and the warehouses with their pointed lofts were locked against an overhung sky that promised snow. The corner where Jack Mahan had sold his papers yesterday was deserted. On the waterfront, Annie washed with freezing water at the public pump next to the horse trough and used the privy at the ferry landing. The tap of her boots on the cobblestones startled her, and without the press of the crowds she felt exposed and unprotected.

She would have liked to have wished Margaret

Hennessy a happy New Year, but instead Annie gave her wishes to a gull standing pink-legged on a nearby piling. The bells on the Seaman's Church struck noon.

A midday ferry, its smoke alive with sparks, crossed the gray river more slowly than usual. Even the boat, Annie thought, was on holiday. At the slip, the horn blasted its arrival, and a crewman jumped onto the wharf and lashed the boat to its mooring. Annie's heart beat a little quicker, and she ran her tongue over her cracked lips.

"A happy New Year to you," she said to the first person off the boat. "And you, too." She held out her hand. "Would it be, madam, that you've seen my brother, Thomas Quinn, blue eyes, fair hair?"

A woman with a sprig of holly on her bonnet shook her head, but she brought a dime out of her fur muff. Behind her two men leading their horses fished in their pockets and pulled out small change. Several people ignored her. An old man gave her two foreign coins. Now the ferry was almost empty, and the rest of the day loomed long and solitary. A dark-skinned girl in a navy cloak and a bonnet hurried onto the landing and dropped a coin in Annie's hand, glanced up, and stopped.

"Annie?" she asked. "Annie. I'm Charlotte Tucker. My mother does the washing for Mrs. Fairchild."

Annie didn't answer but hurried away, her face burning with shame. She'd rather die than talk to this girl.

At the edge of the wharf, Charlotte caught up. "Where have you been?" she asked. "Katherine is so worried."

Annie headed down South Street, but Charlotte kept pace. "Annie. Come home with me."

Annie shook her head and walked faster. She would not be the object of pity. She crossed the street without looking, a dangerous act on any other day.

Charlotte trotted alongside, her words coming out in little puffs. "I promised myself . . . if I ever had another chance . . . I wouldn't let you . . . get away."

Annie broke into a run. But her chest hurt, and her legs were surprisingly slow.

Charlotte pulled Annie to a stop. She urged, "Come home and rest."

Annie studied Charlotte's earnest face and serious eyes, and suddenly she was tired. Her shoulders ached from sleeping on the ground. Her chest was tight with the cold air. She thought about the pistol shots last night, and her resistance crumbled.

"All right," she said. "Just for a few days."

21

Charlotte pushed open the picket gate of the neat frame house off Fulton, and Annie recognized the house as one she had passed any number of times.

"I didn't know you lived here," she said.

"All my life," Charlotte answered. Beside the front door hung a neatly lettered sign, *Tucker Boarding House for Colored Sailors*. A dark-skinned sailor in a heavy peacoat, his pigtail braided tight, paused on his way out the door.

"Good afternoon, Mr. Edwards," Charlotte said. "And happy New Year."

"Good afternoon, Charlotte," the man answered with a hint of a bow.

Charlotte took Annie's arm and led her inside. "Sit here in the parlor while I go tell Mama I found you."

Sunlight streamed through the parlor windows and warmed the wooden captain's chairs and maple tables. Annie tried one of the round-backed chairs, but after so many weeks of sitting with her knees up on the curb or her legs folded Indian-style in her little shed, she felt uncomfortable and restless. She crossed to the mantle above the fireplace and breathed in the evergreen scent of the fresh-cut pine boughs. Clove-studded oranges nestled among the needles. Next to each orange stood a small elephant carved from a pale green stone. Each one slightly larger than the last, the elephants marched in a procession through the oranges. Above the mantle hung the portrait of a broad-faced sailor dressed in a navy coat with gold buttons, a crisp white shirt, and a red scarf whose loose end caught in the breeze. Behind him a foreign harbor bustled with ships and darting yellow birds.

"Is that your father?" Annie asked Charlotte when she came back into the parlor. Annie already knew that the answer must be yes—the man had Charlotte's amber eyes and direct expression.

Charlotte nodded and said, "He had the portrait painted in Cuba two years ago."

"Is he home now?" Annie asked.

"No, he left in September. By now he should be in the East Indies," Charlotte said. She stroked the back of the smallest elephant. "He always brings something back." She gestured around the room at a huge tortoise shell, a trio of vases decorated with elaborate blue flowers, and a freestanding brown globe. Annie moved to see the globe just as Charlotte's mother entered.

"Welcome to our home, Annie," Mrs. Tucker said

and stretched out her hand. If Charlotte had her father's luminous eyes, she also had her mother's oval face, straight back, and full body.

"Mama, didn't I tell you?" Charlotte said. "Annie's nothing but bones. Just like when she first came from Ireland. You've never seen two skinnier strays than Annie and Thomas the first weeks they were at the Fairchilds'."

"Charlotte!"

"But look for yourself."

Mrs. Tucker said, "Annie, please excuse my daughter. She's been worried about you, and now that she's found you, we'd be happy to have you stay a while with us."

Annie dropped a curtsy and noticed her mud-caked boots. "I'd like that, but I have no money." Her mind scrambled for a chore she might do in exchange for lodging, but she could only remember Katherine scolding her for careless housekeeping.

Mrs. Tucker said, "Let's start with a hot bath and something to eat."

Later, after they'd eaten, Charlotte led Annie to the third floor. "Come on," she called over her shoulder. "Mama says we can sleep up here."

Annie followed cautiously up the narrow stairs into a long room lit by dormer windows and crisscrossed with clotheslines. A pair of narrow cots, a common night table, a dresser, and a washstand filled the front part of the room.

"We use this," Charlotte said with a gesture toward the beds, "for extra boarders. The rest," she motioned toward the back, "is the drying room for rainy days."

"Are you sure you won't need the beds?" Annie asked.

Charlotte shook her head. "Winter's our slow time," she said. "Right now, it's just Mr. Edwards on the second floor. He's a sailor and a ship's carpenter. This winter he's working on a clipper at the shipyards, but most of our sailors are at sea in the winter. They leave in the fall for China or the Indies or for whaling in the Pacific. You have to go around the Cape of Good Hope or Cape Horn in summer, you know, when the weather's fair. And it's summer there when we have our winter here." She headed toward the back window. "Come and look!"

Beyond the rooftops, the East River ran deep purple in the dwindling afternoon light. Annie put her hand up to the frosty pane and pressed her finger against a spray of snowflakes caught on the outside of the glass. The first storm of the New Year, she thought, but she was safe inside. She was warm and full and clean, and even, to her surprise, happy.

22

Annie woke to find Charlotte's bed made and the angle of light through the windows announcing mid-morning. Another minute wouldn't hurt, she told herself. She was so comfortable. Cautiously, she stretched her feet down to where the sheets at the bottom of the bed were chilly, but smooth and soft. She could stay here all day, warming up one delicious spot after another, but it was already late enough.

On the second floor, she listened for the sound of sailors, even though Charlotte had said that Mr. Edwards left for work at dawn. Annie had no use for sailors. On the waterfront, they

169

were little help in finding Thomas, and they rarely gave her a penny. They were often so drunk that she stepped off the curb to avoid them. And behind every sailor ashore were memories of the harsh crew, and, worse, the cook on the *Spirit of Liberty.*

In the plain, spotless kitchen at the back of the house, a plate of corn griddlecakes waited for her on the cast-iron stove, and the coffeepot was still warm. She ate in time to the gentle bubbling of the tall soup pot. The sweet scent of carrots and onions escaped under the lid. Annie had forgotten about kitchens, dishes, folded napkins, and simmering soup.

Outside the kitchen window, snow blanketed the ground and edged the top of the back fence, but the steps had been cleared, and a freshly shoveled path led to a small brick building at the end of the yard. Smoke rose from its chimney, and inside someone passed by one of the windows. Hungry for company in a way she hadn't expected, Annie bounded down the back steps, dashed across the yard, pushed open the door, and found Mrs. Tucker doing laundry.

"Good morning, Annie," Mrs. Tucker said through clouds of steam. Her hair was bound in a white turban, and her sleeves were rolled up on smooth, strong arms. She stood at a raised fireplace and ladled hot water from a huge copper kettle into smaller metal buckets. She added kindling to the fire and replenished the kettle from a storage barrel.

"Do you feel strong enough to help?" She pointed to a nearby table piled high with shirts, collars, cuffs, blouses, towels, tablecloths, and napkins. "It wouldn't be too tiring to sort and treat the stains." She reached for a knife, shaved a chunk of soap from a large bar, and handed it to Annie.

"Use soap and hot water directly," Mrs. Tucker said. "This jar of rhubarb is for rust. Lard will take the tar off the bottom of skirts and petticoats. Kerosene draws the grease out of napkins and shirt fronts."

At home, Annie remembered, Mam and she took the clothes down to the river and washed them with soap, if they had any, and laid them out on the grass to dry. If it were rainy, Mam rinsed the dirtiest pieces in the shallow bathing tub and hung them on lines strung across the eaves inside the cottage. No one gave much thought to stains.

Annie set to work sorting, soaping, and rubbing, and soon she was scrubbing and dipping clothes and table linens in and out of pots of water until her fingers had puckered like pale raisins. Nearby, Mrs. Tucker drew a set of sheets from the soaking tub of hot water and moved them to a tub brimming with suds. She hummed while she worked, and everything she did seemed to have an order and a rhythm that was actually restful. Annie thought of Katherine, who cleaned with a determination so fierce that even after the table gleamed, she still returned to rub away some unseen mark.

"Mrs. Tucker," Annie asked, sprinkling a bit of kerosene on a napkin and rubbing the fabric together, "do you think cleanliness is next to godliness?"

"Gracious child," Mrs. Tucker said, "if that were true, I'd be up in heaven right now. I'd be sitting next to Him, and we'd be talking about collars and shirt fronts and gravy stains." She added a mound of tablecloths to the hot water tub and poked them under with a long pole. "No, cleanliness is just for this world. In the end, at our end, the Lord has better ways to judge us than by our laundry."

Mrs. Tucker motioned her over to the sudsing tub with its rising mounds of lather and handed Annie a long stick that ended in a disk with three prongs. "Here, dear," Mrs. Tucker said. "Take this dolly, and move the laundry around from side to side."

Annie stepped onto a wooden box, then carefully lowered the dolly into the soapy water and swished it back and forth. The clothes were heavy under water and hard to move about.

"Don't do more than you can," Mrs. Tucker said, but Annie wasn't about to give up. By midmorning, her arms ached, and Mrs. Tucker had sent her back to sorting. Mrs. Tucker kneaded the laundry one last time and squeezed out the water. She moved everything to the clear rinse water, lifted and squeezed the laundry again, and put it into the copper kettle to boil again.

"We'll leave the shirts to whiten in bleaching powder and hot water. Let's get us some dinner."

Charlotte was already in the kitchen setting the table with soup plates, spoons, and knives. She took one look at Annie's red hands and said, "Annie's been helping with the laundry, hasn't she?"

Mrs. Tucker was almost apologetic. "Well, just a bit."

"Poor Annie," Charlotte said. "Did my mother make you sort for stains?"

Annie nodded.

"And dolly the clothes?" Charlotte pumped an imaginary pole up and down.

Annie nodded again.

"Watch out," Charlotte said. "Next thing, Mama will have you turning the mangle."

"Charlotte," Mrs. Tucker said in a tone that was both warning and exasperation.

"What's a mangle?" Annie asked.

"It's an instrument of torture invented in Spain to break the spirits of young girls," Charlotte said. "At the first saucy word, Spanish mothers set their daughters to the mangle."

"Child," Mrs. Tucker said to Annie, "don't listen to Charlotte. Her head's all filled up with notions. She reads too much."

"You're the one who makes me go to school all four days," Charlotte said, and she laid the soup bowls on the table.

"School?" Annie said the word as if it were in another language.

Charlotte hesitated. "You could go too."

Annie didn't know what to say. Maybe Charlotte thought she hadn't had much schooling. From the laundry lists, Charlotte knew how many words she couldn't spell. But she'd had five years of school and would have kept on, but so many of the students in the little townland school had taken sick or even died from the hunger that the schoolmaster had closed the school and gone to Dublin.

"Oh, we had school at home," Annie said. "Reading and sums, poetry and all. And on South Street, I read the newspaper almost everyday." She thought of Thomas and knew with a shiver that Thomas could barely read at all. "It's Thomas that needs to go to school."

❧

After Charlotte had gone back to her classes, Annie followed Mrs. Tucker to the wash house. "Be careful," Mrs.

Tucker said as she added bleach to the final rinse water. "Too much will turn white clothes gray or streak them with blue."

When the simmering water had cooled, Mrs. Tucker and Annie wrung the laundry out and put it in baskets. Annie reached down but could not lift a basket even an inch from the floor.

"Leave it," Mrs. Tucker called over her shoulder. "You can help me with the sheets."

For the rest of the afternoon, Annie folded sheets and passed them through the rollers of the mangle. She saw what Charlotte meant. The mangle's job was to flatten and press the last bit of water out of sheets and tablecloths. But the system only worked if bricks weighted down the rollers. Mrs. Tucker made it look easy to turn the heavy rollers, but once the bricks were loaded on, Annie couldn't budge the crank. Instead she guided the sheets into the press.

Mrs. Tucker taught her the tune she had been humming that morning. "All day, all night, angels watching over me, my Lord," the two of them sang first together and then as a round. On the third time, Mrs. Tucker broke away from Annie and sang in a lower key, a key that was beautiful and bittersweet to Annie's ears and reminded her of the drone of the pipes at home.

In the yard, Mrs. Tucker lowered the clothesline

strung between the wash house and the kitchen, and Annie threw the laundry along the rope and anchored everything with an army of split wooden clothespins. When the line was up and taunt again, the sheets flapped out like sails, and Annie, her breath like smoke in the cold air, stepped forward into their brilliance. Inside the cone of sparkling white, the world was fresh and pure and smelled of rain and sun and blades of grass. This was the kind of cleanliness that might be next to godliness.

23

Most days, Annie helped Mrs. Tucker with the laundry, and in the evenings, Annie and Charlotte worked at the kitchen table. Charlotte finished her lessons quickly so she could read and memorize poetry, while Annie entered the day's income and expenses into the laundry ledger. Annie enjoyed working out the sums, and Mrs. Tucker had begun to pay her to keep the accounts. And once she had discovered that Annie could also make and repair lace, she paid Annie for that, too.

Sometimes, and always with a touch of guilt, Annie compared the Tucker's home with the Fairchild household. She would never let on to Bridget, but if she had a choice, it would be to stay at the Tuckers'. She worked just as hard for Mrs. Tucker, and in her own way Mrs. Tucker was just as particular as Katherine, but the household was calmer and somehow more hopeful.

"You have to write your mother, you know," Charlotte said one night. "You can't let her think you're still at Gramercy Park."

"But I can't say that I've lost Thomas. It would break her heart. I can't even say I've been looking for him. It's been snowing for days."

"Tell your mother," Charlotte said, "that Bridget has gone away with Mrs. Fairchild and that the two of you have come to live with friends."

Come to live with friends, Annie repeated to herself. *What a wonderful thought. And it wouldn't be too far from the truth.* She said, "I'll write tomorrow."

"Good. I'll correct your spelling."

"Charlotte!"

"Why not? You can't spell."

❧

At night in their beds in the attic, Annie asked, "Why do you read so much? And so much poetry!"

Charlotte rolled over, and the frame gave a squeak. "I'm going to be a poet," she said. In the dark, the bulky hill of Charlotte rose higher as she propped herself up on one elbow. "I'm going to visit England. That's where most poets come from—Shakespeare, Shelley, Lord Byron. And I'm going to be a teacher and a famous speaker."

"And what are you going to talk about?"

"About abolition and the rights of colored people."

Annie said, "Uncle Eamon was always taking about the rights of Irishmen and how the British took them away. But you've had your Revolution, so now you have your rights."

"Yes and no," Charlotte said slowly.

"You and your mother seem fine," Annie said. "You're not. . . "

"No, we're not slaves," Charlotte finished for her. "Our family has been free since my grandparents came here from the West Indies when they were young. But Mama still doesn't have her rights. She cannot ride the omnibus without someone telling her to get off. She cannot have any job she wants. I cannot go to any school but only to the colored school, and it's open only four days a week. And both Mama and I, we have to be careful where we go in the city. Wicked men called 'blackbirds' capture free colored women and girls and sell them down south as slaves."

"Charlotte!" She'd never heard Charlotte speak this way before, so strong and so serious. Unsettling, even disturbing it was. She though of Uncle Eamon and how he could put aside the light and joking part of him. How he could speak to the men who stood in the snow at Lord Cortland's gates and make them feel that he understood their troubles and that he would help them set things right. Charlotte's voice had the same tone, the same promise.

"Have I troubled you, Annie?"

"Troubled me? It's sick with the unfairness of it all, I am. And angry."

"Good. If you're sick and angry, then I'm going to be a fine speaker!"

"Charlotte Tucker, you're impossible!" Annie cried.

"Oooooh," Charlotte said in mock horror. She thumped over in her bed and her dark, nighttime shape curled into a ball under the covers.

⚘

Some nights Annie talked about the hunger. She talked about how the first year the potatoes had seemed fine— the leaves green, the plants full. It was only after the harvest that the whole crop had turned to sludge in the storage pit. Father sold the cow and the chickens and the pig. The neighbors did the same, but soon no one had any money. There was food in Ballinrea but no money to buy it. The British imported Indian meal, and they made up projects like building roads so that everyone would earn the money to buy the meal. Father had become so weak splitting and laying stones that he'd caught the fever and passed away.

"And then Bridget," Annie said, "sent the two tickets, and me and Thomas came over on the *Spirit of Liberty,* and it was the very day we stepped off the ship that Finnbarr O'Halloran stole the fiddle."

"Did you ever try to find it?" Charlotte asked.

"Twice," Annie said. She tucked her hands behind her head and told Charlotte about her visit to Mrs. Gateley's and to Timothy Dunn at the Golden Globe.

"Well, you'll have to go back," Charlotte said.

"I don't have the money."

"I do."

"But you'll be needing it to buy the book of poems you're always sighing over."

"Not anymore," Charlotte confessed. "Mama says Lord Byron is not proper reading for a young girl, and she will not have him in the house. So I might as well lend you the money. Mama doesn't object to music."

❧

Old snow, half-melted and peppered with soot, banked the front of the Golden Globe Pawnshop.

"Ready?" Charlotte asked, her hand on the doorknob.

"Wait," Annie said, but Charlotte opened the door and pulled her in, a small bell ringing their arrival. The first whiff of mildewed clothes and stale food reminded Annie of all the sadness of her first visit.

181

Timothy Dunn's pink and white face appeared from the back of the shop. If he recognized Annie, he didn't show it. "Something to pawn?" he asked.

Charlotte drifted over to the shelf of waterlogged books, and Annie summoned up her courage. "I've come for my fiddle," she said. "The one Finnbarr O'Halloran pawned last July. I have the money now."

"It's no use, miss," Timothy Dunn said. "O'Halloran came in last week, paid up, and took it away. Something about how he'd been in a barroom fight at Jimmy Healey's, thrown a stool, missed the other gentleman, and hit the fiddle player." He rustled the pages of his ledger. "Here you are." He turned the ledger so Annie could see the spidery writing. *Number 178. Handmade violin and case, pawned July 5, 1847. $3.50. Redeemed February 20, 1848.*

Annie fought the sinking, bottomless feeling of disappointment. "Do you know," she asked, "where I might find Finnbarr?"

Timothy Dunn passed his hand over his hair. "Tough place, Healey's is. One of the worst at the Points. Thinks he's a big shot, O'Halloran does—dropping names like Jimmy Healey's."

"I'm going round there," Annie said to Charlotte as they left the shop.

"You can't!"

"We'll go together."

"Oh, no!" Charlotte said, "I'm not going near the Five Points."

"Fine. I'll go alone." Annie pulled the door open and headed to the street.

"Wait!" Charlotte called. "You're running off again. You need a plan."

"I *have* a plan," Annie called back. "I'm going to find Finnbarr O'Halloran and make him tell me where to find Thomas."

☙

"The Five Points, sir?" Annie asked the first gentleman she saw.

"Not the place for a young girl," the man said, shaking his head as if he might have a daughter her age.

"It's my brother, Thomas, I'm after."

"Irish," the man said, his voice a little cooler. "Well, take Center Street and turn left on Anthony. When you get to the little park, you're at the Points."

"Thank you, sir," Annie said and curtsied. She refused the coin he offered, and he seemed puzzled.

Anthony Street ended in a free-for-all. Carriages and carts careened around the corners. Wagons and cabs sped from side streets directly into traffic. Horses churned the dirt and snow into slush, and puddles the size of thawing lakes stretched between the street and sidewalk. Annie held up her skirts and threaded her way to the policeman in the little park.

"Sir," she asked, "I'm looking for Jimmy Healey's tavern."

The policeman lifted his chin and ran his finger between his thick neck and tight collar. He waved his nightstick over the rush of traffic to the dingy shops across the street. "Take your pick," he said. "They're all taverns."

Annie dodged back the way she'd come, sidestepping grinding wheels, horses' hooves, and cursing drivers. On the sidewalk again, she gingerly edged around the long legs of a beggar slumped against a wall. A handbill proclaiming *Christy's Minstrels—Tenth Straight Week on Broadway*, blew against his side. In front of a dance hall, a street barker set three shells on top of a table with two broken legs that had been tied together by string.

"See the bean, see the bean," the barker cried. "Find the bean and double your money."

Two sailors—one long as a rail with a pockmarked face, the other short with a chest like a seaman's trunk—stumbled out of a dance hall with arms around each other's shoulders. They paused to watch. The tall one put down a coin, and the bean man made the shells fly until they came to rest again in a perfect line.

"The middle one," Annie whispered to herself.

The wide sailor pointed to the middle shell, and Annie leaned forward. With a flourish, the bean man picked the shell up—no bean! Annie blinked with surprise and disappointment. The bean man raised the shell on his right, and the bean, small and speckled, rocked gently in its place. The sailors stomped away. The bean man swept the coin off the tabletop and called, "See the bean. See the bean."

Annie didn't stay to watch another game. At a grocery on the corner, a black woman with a wiry tangle of gray hair clicked off the stitches on a sleeve while her customers rummaged through the bins of cabbage, apples, and turnips.

"Jimmy Healey's tavern?" Annie asked.

The woman finished her row and pointed the free needle across the way. "Ask at the Old Brewery."

With a sinking heart, her toes turning to ice inside her boots, Annie crossed another flooded street to the derelict building the woman had called the Old Brewery. Only the mounds of garbage piled against the walls seemed to keep it upright. On the front stoop a young woman in a tattered cloak drank from a bottle. Despite the cold, her face was flushed.

"Do you know Jimmy Healey's tavern?" Annie asked. "It's Finnbarr O'Halloran and my brother, Thomas, I'm hoping to find."

The young woman looked up in surprise, knocked the door behind her ajar and called, "Thomas, your sister's here."

Annie held her breath. The door swung back, and a man stumbled out.

"Here, now, Thomas," the woman said. "It's your sister come to find you." The man smiled at Annie, his eyes watery and bloodshot. He lurched forward and gripped her shoulder.

"No," Annie cried and pulled away. "No!"

The woman shrieked with laughter. "Come now," she said, "is that any way to greet a brother?"

Blindly, Annie ran into the puddles and across the street. Her heart thumped like a kettledrum.

24

"I can't ask him," Annie said and drew her quilt up to her chin. She'd been shivering ever since she'd come home from the Points, her clothes soaked and shoes so wet the toes curled. Even in bed now, dry and warm, her teeth still wanted to chatter.

"It's not 'can't,'" Charlotte said, "it's 'won't.'"

"I can't."

"But why not, Annie?"

"I've already told you. Because."

"Mr. Edwards knows the city. He can walk into Jimmy Healey's and ask for Finnbarr and for Thomas, just as if he were looking for a mate from his ship."

Annie had to admit this was true. No one would look twice at Mr. Edwards or bother him. And as an old friend of Charlotte's father, he'd do anything for the family.

"Is it because he's colored?" Charlotte asked.

Annie sat up in bed. "Is that what you think?"

"Well, maybe. You wouldn't be the first person."

"Charlotte Tucker!" Annie sprinted barefoot across the unheated room. "Move over! I'm coming to shake that idea right out of you."

"No room! I'll roll off!"

"No room?" Annie scoffed. "At home Bridget and me and sometimes Norah shared a bed half the size of this one. And the cat crawled on top of us and lay there like a stone."

"Ow!" Charlotte wailed. "Keep your feet away. They're like icebergs."

"Well, no more comments, or I'll iceberg you."

"So, what are you waiting for? Ask Mr. Edwards! Do it for me."

Annie leaned against the rail at the head of the bed and tucked the toes of one foot under the instep of the other. "Charlotte Tucker, you are one of the finest people I know."

"Last week you said I was the bossiest person you knew."

Annie ignored her. "If it hadn't been for you, I'd still be out on the waterfront. It's you who helped me write home. You're the one who made me go to Timothy Dunn's, and now we know where to find Finnbarr."

"So will you ask?'

"I'll think about it."

"About time," Charlotte said. She flopped over and was soon asleep.

Annie sat very still and tried to imagine asking Mr.

Edwards. She saw herself stepping up to him as he smoked his pipe or practiced his knots in the parlor, but she couldn't hear herself say the words. It wasn't that she was afraid. Mr. Edwards wasn't a man to be afraid of. It was something else, something she couldn't explain.

Later that night, she dreamed of the Old Brewery. This time it wasn't a building at the Five Points, but a ship with sailors who leaned out the windows, pointed, and laughed at her. They threw buckets of water out of the windows, and the water poured past her to form wide, silvery puddles on the sidewalk. From deep in the building, Annie heard Thomas calling her, but when she started in the door, the ship's cook came toward her. His open mouth drooled, the scar on his cheek twisted, and the pupils of his eyes burned in a fiery web.

♣

Annie saved the dusting for the afternoons when Mrs. Tucker was ironing. She liked to take her time, hold the great tortoise shell in both hands, trace her finger over the vines and flowers on the china vase. Sometimes she peeked into the guest registry and read out loud the names of the sailors, their home port, job, and most recent ship.

"Nat Pell, Jamaica, seaman, the *Freedom*. Hosea Brown, Nantucket, harpooner, the *Sarah and Julia*. Isaac

Edwards, Antigua, able seaman, the *Samuel Pennington*."

With her fingertips, she walked her way around the freestanding globe, finding the sailors' homes. Jamaica, she discovered, was an island and so were Antigua and Nantucket. They were all islands, just like Ireland. Funny, she thought, she and the sailors were island people. They had that in common.

Slowly, she turned the globe and looked for other islands. There was Australia, where Father had said the British sent Irish patriots. Look how far away it was! And how big! At home, before she'd ever seen a globe or even a map, she'd thought Ireland was very large and Australia and even America very small. Now she saw that Ireland was almost nothing, a small robin's egg in the sea. And yet Ireland was everything, because it was home.

The door behind her creaked, and Annie flew to the mantel. Mr. Edwards came in, settled himself in the chair by the window, and unfolded his copy of the *Maritime News*.

"Excuse me, sir," she said and curtsied. "I'm almost finished."

"You needn't go, Annie," Mr. Edwards said. He put away his newspaper and took out a length of rope and a tapered metal tool. He looped and threaded the rope until an elaborate knot appeared almost by magic. With a poke of his marlinespike, the knot unraveled and the rope straightened.

Annie pulled her eyes away from the rope and gestured toward the elephants. She said, "Just dusting these."

"Do you like them?"

"Please, sir?"

"The elephants."

Annie dropped a second curtsy, and said, "Oh, yes, sir."

"The thing about green," Mr. Edwards said, deep in thought, while Annie stood motionless at the fireplace. "I've seen jade in China, emeralds in India, marble in Italy. The ocean itself has endless shades of green."

"Yes, sir." Annie said.

"But the most beautiful green," Mr. Edwards continued, "is Ireland. Did you know that, Annie?"

"Yes, sir. I mean, no, sir."

"In your country, even the sunlight is a glorious green."

"Thank you, sir."

Mr. Edwards set aside the rope and took out his pipe and tobacco. On the back of his hand, the tattooed eagle fluttered while he tamped the tobacco into the pipe, struck a match, and sucked the flame deep into the bowl.

"And your people," he said, "are some of the finest on earth." He leaned back and blew out the first sweet puffs of smoke. "Did you know that, Annie?"

"Yes, sir. I mean, thank you, sir." Annie moved toward the door, but Mr. Edwards held out his pipe, the bowl cradled in his palm. He looked at her with a concentration that caught her as tight as one of his knots.

"I was crew on the *Aurelia* out of Liverpool last year," he said, never taking his eyes off her. "We had three times the passengers we could safely carry. Ten days out of port, the fever hit like a wildfire. At the worst of it, the captain drove everyone below decks and locked the hatch. For more than a week, he ordered his sailors to lower food and water down in a bucket. A braver, more courageous group in steerage I've never seen. "

"Yes, sir," Annie said.

"I have nightmares still."

"I appreciate your saying so, sir." Annie felt her cheeks blaze and rushed to correct herself. "Not about the nightmares, sir. I mean about us, sir, the Irish." Annie curtsied and fled.

Outside the room, she pressed against the wall to catch her breath. *A braver, more courageous group.... Some of the finest people on earth.* Mr. Edwards was talking about her people. He was talking about her. She knew that in his own way, he was telling her not to judge all sailors by the few she had seen. Not every sailor taunted the Irish or ignored their suffering.

And if she were brave and if she were courageous, she would understand that. And she would also understand that there was nothing wrong in asking for help. She straightened her apron and knocked on the door.

"Mr. Edwards," Annie said, "It's a bit of help I'm needing. Thomas, my brother, is at Jimmy Healey's at the Five Points, and I can't be finding him on my own. If it wouldn't be too much, if you had some time . . . "

Mr. Edwards put up his hand. "Come in, Annie," he said, his voice grave and his eyes full of concern. "Come in and tell me about your brother."

25

From a distance, Annie saw Margaret Hennessy, the sweet potato lady, tipping the ashes out of her kettle. She called out. "Mrs. Hennessy!"

"Who's that, Granny?" a dark-haired little girl asked and pulled on the old woman's skirt.

Annie crossed South Street to the ferry landing and said, "I'm Annie Quinn." She noticed the girl's sea-green eyes. "And you'd be Norah."

"Norah Mahan," the little girl announced. "I'm

four." She looked at her palm, folded her thumb inward, and held up her fingers. "Four."

Annie couldn't help smiling. "And your brother is Jack?"

Norah nodded. "He's thirteen." She spread her ten fingers wide, turned her thumbs in, then out, made small fists and jammed them behind her. "Thirteen."

"Well," Annie said, "I have a little sister named Norah and three brothers."

"Where are they?" Norah asked and looked around.

Margaret Hennessy said, "Jack was just talking about you a few nights ago, wondering where you'd gone. He was worried, you being so young and so thin."

Annie flushed with surprise.

"I've been living with friends," she said, amazed at how easily the word slipped out. "I help with the laundry and housework."

Margaret Hennessy glanced at Annie's clean cloak and bonnet, both castoffs from Charlotte, and nodded her approval. "It's good friends you got. You're not so thin now, and you've a bit of color too. And your brother, did you find him?"

Annie shook her head. "It's Finnbarr we've found," she said. "And Thomas might be with him." She stopped because this was the hard part. "Mr. Edwards will help, but we'll be needing a cart. I was hoping. Well, Mr.

Hennessy. If he would."

"Wait a bit, dear," the old woman said, "and you can ask him yourself."

"Daisy," Norah cried and pointed to the horse and refuse wagon just turning off South Street. The wagon drew to a halt, and Dan Hennessy jumped to the cobblestones.

"How's me Norah?" he said, lifting the girl to his shoulders. "How's me pretty cailín?"

Norah giggled, clutched at his ears, and pointed to Annie. "She's got a Norah, too."

"Grand to see you, miss," Hennessy said. He set Norah on the ground and held out a rough hand. "Found your brother, yet?"

Dan Hennessy, Annie thought. *Ellen's Uncle Daniel!* Annie explained that she had come over from Ireland with William and Ellen. The Hennessys told her that the O'Sheas were fine.

William made hats, and Ellen worked in an umbrella factory. They had found a set of rooms near their shops on the West Side.

"I've no love for Finnbarr O'Halloran," Dan Hennessy said when Annie explained about the fiddle and Thomas running away and her being thrown out of Gramercy Park. "Three minutes of his talk and you're turning out your pockets, begging him to take your money." He grew serious. "I'd like to teach him a lesson."

26

In her sailor's rough trousers and shirt, her shoulder-length hair pulled into a pigtail, Annie hoped she looked enough like a boy to pass for Mr. Edward's young assistant. She put a bit of a roll into her gait and stared back at the drunks who staggered between grog shops and taverns at the Five Points. Mr. Edwards walked by her side, and Dan Hennessy came behind them in his wagon.

Around the corner from the Old Brewery, Mr. Edwards signaled Hennessy to wait in the alley and motioned Annie to follow him into a dark tavern. The air reeked of smoke, and the floor was slick with beer. Annie choked back a cough—a ship's boy spent his days around tobacco smoke. Mr. Edwards sent Annie over to a table, and he went to the narrow bar to order.

The few sailors already there wrapped their hands around their drinks and ignored the newcomers. Annie leaned her elbows on the sticky table and tried to remember how Thomas sat. Without skirts, she felt different—freer. She arranged herself with her legs apart, her body forward, and one hand pressed down on her knee.

Mr. Edwards brought over two smudged tumblers.

"Drink up," he said in a hearty voice. Annie raised her mug of beer and almost missed the two figures who slipped in the door and headed down the stairs behind the bar.

"Thomas and Finnbarr!" she whispered to Mr. Edwards.

"Wait here," Mr. Edwards said, and he headed outside to alert Dan Hennessy.

Annie couldn't wait. She couldn't have Thomas slip away again. Just a bit of a glance told her that he was thinner than ever and still in the same clothes he'd worn when he left Gramercy Place. Only now they were rags.

Annie pushed back her chair and headed after Thomas. At the bottom of the stairs, tallow candles barely lit the basement hallway. Muffled shouts pulled her further into the gloom until she stopped at the far end of the corridor.

"Blessed Mother," she murmured in prayer and turned the knob.

A gust of air, cold as winter and raw as sewage, swept her into a room swarming with ragged boys. They wrestled on the floor, tugged at each other's heads, pounded backs, punched, and twisted an arm or shoulder. Their eyes were dull, and their hair hung long and matted about their sooty faces. Some of the boys circled and chased each other around a waist-high metal tub in the center of the room.

A long chute led from the tub to an open grate high on the wall. Outside in the alley, a boy poked his head through the square and said, "Watch out, she's coming down!"

The boys stopped their horseplay and looked up. High-pitched shrieks and a frantic skittering of claws ran the length of the shoot, and something thick and soft tumbled into the metal tub. The boys erupted in cheers and whistles. Two men—deep in conversation—entered from an adjoining room. One was broad-shouldered with a heavy beard and a pistol in his waistband.

The other was Finnbarr O'Halloran.

He would notice her for sure, Annie thought, but she couldn't leave without seeing Thomas. If only she could tell him that Mr. Edwards and Ellen's Uncle Dan were here to help him escape. But Thomas was hard to find. The room was small and tightly packed, and in the half-light all the boys looked the same, as if they were thieves in a bandit's den.

"Thomas," Finnbarr cried, "pick us a champion."

Thomas edged his way forward. His hair fell almost to his shoulders, and his blue eyes were bright in a face streaked by grime. He studied the tub, plunged in his hands, and quickly pulled up a huge, gray rat. Its red eyes bulged, and its long and clawlike feet splayed out, thrashed for a grip on the air.

"Aye, Thomas!" someone shouted. "He's a winner!"

Queasy with the stink of the room and the size of the rat, Annie slipped out the door. Mr. Edwards met her at the bottom of the stairs. He didn't scold her for going off, but only asked, "Thomas?"

Annie pointed to the end of the corridor.

"Hennessy is in the alley," Mr. Edwards said. "If anything goes wrong, run to meet him." He paused before a door labeled, *Healey's Sporting Parlor.* "Ready, mate?"

"Aye, sir." Annie said, her voice weak and unconvincing.

Mr. Edwards pushed his way through the crowd and toward a circle of branches around a sunken pit heavily strewn with sawdust. The room was filled with men talking and drinking. A sullen-faced boy came through a low gate into the sunken pit and raked the sawdust evenly from edge to edge while Mr. Edwards found two seats on the front row.

"Place your bets. Place your bets!" Finnbarr O'Halloran's voice rang out somewhere behind Annie. "Last chance! Last chance to be a winner!" He stopped at Annie's row, his knees right beside her.

Mr. Edwards reached into his pocket and said, "Make it three for Edwards."

"Grand," Finnbarr said, and he patted Annie's shoulder without looking at her. "Brought your cabin boy along, eh? Never too early." Annie stared down at her shoes, not daring to move a muscle.

"That's right," Mr. Edwards said, and Finnbarr's knees and shoes headed back up the aisle.

The crowd erupted into a roar and Annie raised her head. Two boys with matching metal boxes had come into the pit. One was Thomas. They lifted the hinged lids at the end of each box and jumped back on the other side of the gate. Four rats and a brown-and-white dog burst into the small arena.

"Thomas!" Annie cried over the shouts of the men around her. "Thomas! Thomas!"

At the sound of his name, Thomas looked up. His eyes widened and he mouthed, "Annie!"

In the pit, the barking terrier cornered two of the rats and lunged. The rats rolled over, staggered up, and blood stained the sand. Thomas shouted to Annie and pointed toward a door behind him. The little dog wheeled, snapped, and flung something heavy across the pit. The crowd exploded.

"I'll bring Thomas outside," Mr. Edwards said in Annie's ear. "Meet us in the alley."

He pushed his way around the ring and toward the door where Thomas had disappeared. Annie fought her way down the aisle only to find the way out blocked by Finnbarr O'Halloran.

"Miss Roscommon! How pleasant to see you again. You've the makings of a fine sailor."

Annie glared at him. "Excuse me."

"Why not stay longer? Why not place a bet? Which do you favor, rats or dogs?" Finnbarr never raised his voice, never changed his mocking tone even though the noise around them grew louder.

"O'Halloran." The bearded man with the pistol stepped from the darkness. "Where are the other rats? Where's the boy in charge of the rats? The men aren't going to wait all day."

"I'll fetch him, Healey," said Finnbarr.

Annie tried to slip around Finnbarr while he was distracted, but he grabbed her arm and pulled her with him into the hallway. He hurried toward the rat room. Annie struggled, but the harder she pulled, the tighter he gripped her arm. She went limp, a dead weight. She dug in her heels and made him drag her along. He gave a yank, and she rushed forward.

Finnbarr staggered off balance, and she kicked him in the back of the knees. Finnbarr thrust out both hands to break his fall, and Annie raced up the stairs.

"Oh, no, you don't," Finnbarr cried, and his heavy boots drummed behind her—out of the tavern, down the alley. Ahead of her, Dan Hennessy held Thomas while Mr. Edwards wrapped him in a rug.

"He's a fighter, your brother is," Hennessy called.

"Finnbarr!" Annie shouted.

"Right!" Hennessy cried. He released Thomas, sprang like a lion, and caught Finnbarr in his arms.

"They're taking me away!" Thomas called to Annie. His head bobbed out the end of the carpet roll as Mr. Edwards loaded him onto the wagon. "Help!"

Annie wanted to laugh, but she was already crying and panting for breath.

"It's a rescue, Thomas," she said. "Mr. Hennessy, he's Ellen's uncle, and Mr. Edwards, he's Charlotte Tucker's friend. They've saved you."

The two men tied Finnbarr's wrists and ankles and pushed him onto the wagon beside Thomas.

"Blackguard!" Hennessy said to Finnbarr. "I'll think of something. I've time. It's a long ride to Harlem we've got."

Mr. Edwards helped Annie onto the wagon. He said, "I'll tell Mrs. Tucker we found Thomas and that you're headed uptown."

"Thank you, Mr. Edwards," Annie said. "Without you—" She would have said more, but Mr. Edwards, standing beside the wagon, shook his head and slapped Daisy on the rump. The wagon lurched forward. Annie grabbed Thomas to be sure he didn't roll off, and Finnbarr braced himself with his feet.

"Hie there!" Hennessy shouted and, with surprising spirit, Daisy turned the corner and barreled through the traffic at the Five Points.

27

From the back of the wagon, the city dropped farther and farther away until the brick row houses separated into low-roofed farms, and the cobbled streets became plank roads and dirt tracks through open fields. The upturned earth gave the air a freshness that reminded Annie of home, and above the low hills, the evening star glimmered in the violet sky. *Bring us all together,* she wished, as she always did. *Bring us together in New York.*

"Where are we?" Finnbarr called to Hennessy.

"Out in the country," Hennessy shouted over his shoulder.

"Looks more like Ireland," Finnbarr said in a tone of disapproval. From the crest of the road, a cluster of kerosene lights winked below in the windows of the shantytown. The cart jostled onto a rutted lane and a clutch of chickens cackled and sprang away. Dan Hennessy pulled Daisy to a stop before a lopsided wooden house.

"Go on inside," he said to Annie and Thomas. "They're expecting you."

Annie hopped down and helped Thomas, now free

of the rug, off the wagon.

"What about me?" Finnbarr said.

"Eh," Hennessy said, "you can go back now." He untied Finnbarr and helped him off the wagon.

"Back?" Finnbarr asked. He stood rubbing his wrists.

"Aye."

"But it's all country, all empty it is, " he said. He gestured to the thick woods beyond the road, the patches of snow under the leafless tree trunks, and the darkening road beyond the cabins.

"'Tis," agreed Hennessy.

"And no omnibus. No cabs."

"For sure. Not a one. But it's a grand night. The moon will be up soon, and not much chance of bears."

"Bears?" Finnbarr hiccuped.

Annie held back her laughter.

"Ah, well," Hennessy said. "Maybe a few. But not many. It's early still."

In the dwindling light, Finnbarr's face was ashen, and his jaw fell slack.

"Better get on then," Hennessy said, nodding toward the road. "And if you ever bother Annie or Thomas again, it will be the Catskill Mountains for you. A real walk in the country that is."

"And after all I've done for Thomas," Finnbarr said, sounding genuinely hurt and unappreciated.

"Off with you," Hennessy growled.

Finnbarr jammed his hands in his pockets, hunched his shoulders against the evening chill, and set off along the lane. His stovepipe hat against the purple clouds was the last thing of him to disappear back down the road in the direction of the city.

❧

Norah Mahan pulled open the cabin door. Without any other greeting to Annie, she said, "Did you bring your Norah?"

"Come in, both of ye," Margaret Hennessy called from the hearth. Thomas stepped into the little house, and Jack Mahan peeled Norah away from Annie's leg and shook Thomas's hand.

"So. My missing twin is it? Ah, now, for sure you're the better-looking one."

Annie blushed at the difference between the two boys. Beyond the fair hair, the boys looked nothing alike. Jack was taller than Annie remembered, and his face had more planes and angles, his nose was straight, and his jaw square. No one would have ever confused one boy for the other.

Jack and Norah and Thomas found stools in front of the fire while Margaret poured tumblers of milk and passed a basket of potatoes. At first there were only the

sounds of "please," and "thanks," and "pass the creel."
Annie sat beside Thomas and, when she was sure he'd
eaten enough, she asked him all the questions she'd
been saving.

"Thomas, what happened after Mr. Belzer hit you?
Where did you go?"

Thomas pushed his hair out of his eyes. "At first I
just ran. Halfway to Pearl Street I was before I had to
stop. I figured that if I went back to the Fairchilds', for
sure Mr. Belzer would beat me. So I kept walking all the
way to the waterfront. And I had this idiot idea that I
could join a fire company."

Margaret Hennessy banged the fire tongs on the
brick hearth.

"I thought Finnbarr could help me, so I went round
to Mrs. Gateley's, and he was happy to see me. He
remembered you too, Annie. 'Miss Roscommon,' he
called you."

Annie wanted to say what she had privately called
Finnbarr O'Halloran, but it might upset Thomas, who
had clearly been through enough.

"Once I was in with Finnbarr," Thomas said, "I got
confused. He took me to Barnum's Museum, and we saw
the Feejee Mermaid—twice! And he was a grand one for
schemes. He had me stop gentlemen in the street and
ask directions, and while I was asking, he took purses out

of their pockets. He had me pick up the bags of passengers at the docks without asking and carry them off to Mrs. Gateley's. And he said I was the best helper he'd ever had. And he always gave me a part of the money—it's in my shoe. I saved it to buy tickets for Mam."

Annie winced at the thought of ship's passage bought with stolen money.

"How did you end up at the Five Points?" Jack asked.

"Finnbarr had an argument with Mrs. Gateley, something about him stealing her fancy dishes," Thomas said.

"And she kicked you out," Annie said. "I came the next day, but you'd already gone.

Thomas nodded. "Mrs. Gateley made us leave, and Finnbarr heaved a brick through her window, and she said she'd have the police on us, and we'd spend the winter at Sing Sing Prison. I was scared, but Finnbarr just laughed and said he had a friend, Jimmy Healey, what owned a grog shop, and he'd look after us."

"And it was at Healey's you were living?" Annie asked.

Thomas shook his head, and his hair fell back into his eyes. "We lived with the other boys in a room at the Old Brewery. Me and my friends collected the rats for Healey. Ten cents a rat we got and a big swig of whiskey. We'd go hunting at night, sleep a couple of hours, then come in and work the parlor."

"The room with the grate on the window and the

chute," Annie said, "what was that?"

"You saw the holding room?" Thomas asked. Annie nodded. "A grand system, Jimmy Healey has." Thomas puffed a bit with pride. "You bring the rats around through the alley in a sack and empty them into the chute, and they slide down into a collecting pen. The chute and the pen are lined with tin, so the rats can't chew their way out."

"Ah, now, Thomas," Annie said, sad beyond words at the life he'd been leading and the way he looked. With dark circles under his eyes and hollow cheeks, he was as haggard as he'd been coming off the *Spirit of Liberty* last summer.

Thomas went on. "I tried to tell you where I was. A couple of times, early in the morning, I came up to see you at Gramercy Park. The first time, Martin Belzer wouldn't let me in the house. The next time, I got as far as the kitchen, but Mrs. Cox said that you'd been let go for stealing and that if I didn't leave, she'd call a policeman."

"Did you see Katherine?"

"No," Thomas said and looked puzzled. "She wouldn't have helped me."

Annie said, "Aye. She would have."

Thomas shrugged. "Healey had a pistol, and he kept a close eye on us. When I saw you at the pit, I thought it was a dream. The next thing, some sailor's breaking me arm, twisting it around behind me back."

"Oh, Thomas," Annie said, "that was Mr. Edwards. He's a friend of the Tuckers." She started at the beginning and explained how she had been dismissed from Gramercy Place and gone to live on the waterfront, how she had met Jack and the Hennessys and moved in with Charlotte Tucker.

"And the man who grabbed me with the knife? He was a friend of the girl who takes in the Fairchilds' laundry?" Thomas asked, uncertain.

Annie nodded, "That was Mr. Edwards, and it wasn't a knife. It was just the tool he uses for separating rope and making knots. He'll show you when we go back to Charlotte's."

"Do I have to go?" Thomas asked and looked around. "Can't I stay here, at least for a little while?" He ducked his head. "It's nice here."

Margaret Hennessy said, "I don't know why the poor child couldn't stay."

Dan Hennessy came in the door in time to hear his wife's invitation. "Annie tells me you've a way with horses," he said to Thomas. "I know some fellows up here could use a hand."

"Annie?" Margaret Hennessy said. "What about you? There's room for you too. Won't you stay with us, at least until your sister comes home? William and Ellen come up of a Sunday, and they would love to see you."

"You can sleep with me," Norah said.

"And you'd be with your own kind," Hennessy said.

Irish, he means, Annie thought. *But what about Charlotte?* She and Annie were a kind, too. They were as close as sisters, closer than she and Bridget had ever been. Charlotte looked after her and made her plan ahead. At night, in the attic bedroom, Charlotte rambled on about things she could never tell her mother, how she was half in love with the poet Lord Byron, how she was going to travel, to be a writer and a teacher, and to speak out against slavery and injustice to women. The Hennessys were Irish, her kind, but Charlotte was her friend.

"May I spend the night?" she asked. "But I have to go back to the Tuckers'. I have work to do there."

"Of course," Hennessy said, but he looked disappointed.

Norah brought over her rag doll, dropped it into Annie's lap, and pointed out her baby's button eyes and embroidered nose and mouth. She leaned back, and Annie was happy to cradle a small sister again.

"There was a man out walking," Dan Hennessy said, starting a story, "and it got on to evening. And the man was far from home. And the road was a lonely one. But he had a ways to go, so he walked on. And it was cold, you know. At last he could go no farther, so he looked for a place to lie down, even if it were only by the side of the road.

"And, don't you know, it was an odd thing, but right then he saw a small cottage. And the door was open. So he went in and the fire was lit and the house was warm. He lay down by the hearth and fell asleep. In the morning, he woke up and looked around. And he even called out, 'Anyone home?' But no one answered.

"And he called again, 'Anyone home?' Only silence. The house was empty. And he couldn't wait much longer. So he set out. And he went up the road, and at the top of the hill, he looked back.

"It was one last glance at the cottage he was wanting. And everywhere he looked, it was only wild land. There was not a trace of the house or even the smoke from the chimney or any other dwelling anywhere."

Hennessy fell quiet. Thomas and Jack studied the fire, and Norah, her head nodding, leaned against Annie. This house—these people—wouldn't vanish, Annie promised herself. And she'd hold on to her friendship with Charlotte. She wouldn't let any of them disappear.

28

Annie let herself into the Tuckers' on Sunday morning, eager to share her adventures, but Charlotte and her mother had already gone to church. A letter from Mam lay on the table.

Annie opened it quickly, her fingers fumbling on the pasted flap. Inside, the news was more than two months old.

December, 1847
Dear Annie and Thomas,
    I hope that you are well and managing at the Fairchilds' even while Bridget is away.

Her mother believed that she and Thomas were still at Gramercy Park. The letter Charlotte had helped her write in January was just now arriving in Ireland, and already it was March. Annie read on:

This has been a hard winter, but we have been lucky so far. Hugh McDermott helped us break into Eamon's shed, so we have a roof over our heads and are dry and out of the cold. On my last visit to the jail in Ballinrea, Eamon told me to sell everything and buy food for ourselves.

"No one starves in jail," he said. He has saved our lives, and I pray his own will be spared. The charge against him is attempted murder, and rumor has it that Peter Reilly has been paid handsomely to testify against him.

Last week Mr. Denby announced that his Lordship is providing us and all the neighbors in the townland with passage, come Saint Patrick's Day, to Montreal or New York. For sure we can't help but think of the McDermott girls and the others lost on that terrible ship last summer. Still, I remember that Bridget bought your tickets on the Black Star Line, so I will tell Mr. Denby to book us places on one of those ships. You will have to ask at the shipping office in New York the date of arrival for ships leaving Ireland in early spring.

If anyone had told me five years ago that I would give up this dear land, I would have laughed out loud. Now the townland is mostly empty, all our old friends and family have died or gone into exile. The fields are overgrown. The cottages are but piles of stone and thatch, and barely a soul travels the road. This place I've known from my first steps now feels as foreign as the moon. Only the thought that we will soon be together eases my sadness.

Your loving,

Mam

Annie slipped the letter back into its envelope and tried not to think how difficult the trip would be for Mam. How would she manage with the storms, the fever, the raw and wormy food, the noise belowdeck, the constant crying of children? Annie thought of home, with its paths and fields, the fairy fort, the turf bogs, and the scattered cottages empty and abandoned. She pulled her shawl closer. Outside, the sunlight caught and warmed the first pale shoots on the ailanthus tree.

"Annie?" Charlotte called from the front door. She burst into the kitchen. "Mr. Edwards won't tell me a thing! Promise you'll give me every detail. If only I could have been there."

Mrs. Tucker tied on her apron. With an exasperated glance at her daughter she said, "Annie, don't listen to that girl. These days she goes on and on. You've got more sense than two of her. Now help me roll out the biscuits. We've got new boarders expecting Sunday dinner."

"Do you want to hear my news?" Charlotte whispered as she counted out the silverware. "When I took the laundry up to Gramercy Park, while you were at the Points, Katherine gave me your letter and told me that Mrs. Fairchild and Bridget are coming back next Friday."

"So soon?" Annie asked. She was excited and afraid. What would happen, she wondered, if she and Thomas were not at the house when Bridget returned? "What am I going to do?"

Charlotte pointed upstairs, and Annie understood. They'd talk about it later.

❀

"What am I to do?' Annie asked again when at last Charlotte and she were sitting cross-legged on Charlotte's bed.

"Well, what's the problem?"

"You know the problem," Annie tried not to shout.

"Well, then, use the Tucker method."

If you have a problem, Charlotte had instructed Annie more than once, go over the whole situation and ask what you want to happen in the end. When you know the problem and the solution, you can begin looking for the key.

"And the key," Charlotte reminded Annie, "isn't always what you expect. Take Lord Byron. I've been asking for Byron's poetry all winter, the complete works with the gilt-edged pages, but Mama says, 'No.'" Charlotte wagged her finger in a stern imitation of her mother. "She thinks it's not suitable for young girls. Mama's never going to let me buy Lord Byron, not even the smallest, plainest copy. But she does let me go to the lending library."

"Charlotte!" Annie said, horrified that anyone would go behind the back of a woman as kind as Mrs. Tucker.

For a moment, Charlotte looked uncomfortable, but she went on, her chin up, her tone defiant. "So the library is the key. I read Lord Byron a little at a time each week at the library." She ran her finger along the stitching on her quilt. "Mama's right. Some of those poems are not for young girls—but they're still wonderful!"

Annie shook her head. Who was she to say what

Charlotte should do or tell her mother? After all, hadn't she lied to Mam that Thomas and she had Bridget's permission to live with the Tuckers.

She slipped off the bed and paced the attic. "So, here's the problem," Annie said as much to herself as to Charlotte. "Mrs. Fairchild is coming home next week, and right away Mrs. Cox will say that Thomas ran off because Martin Belzer saw him setting fires and that she sacked me for stealing. Bridget will argue it's not true, and Mrs. Fairchild won't know whom or what to believe. Since Mrs. Cox and Martin Belzer are her husband's servants, she might let Bridget go in order to be free of all us Quinns."

"Think," Charlotte said. "Use the Tucker method. And don't say you'll run around the neighborhood asking total strangers for help."

Annie swatted Charlotte's arm. "I'm not a total goose!"

"No, now you're a goose with a bit more common sense."

"Charlotte!" Annie raised her fist.

"No, no!" Charlotte cried. "I was wrong. You're a brave and courageous goose, and you've every bit as much common sense as the next...goose."

"That's better," Annie laughed.

Charlotte pressed on. "Go back to the problem and

think how you found Thomas."

Annie spoke slowly. "I found Thomas, or rather, we found Thomas by talking to Timothy Dunn."

"And who was Timothy Dunn?"

Annie looked at Charlotte in disbelief, and Charlotte raised her eyebrows, expecting an answer. Annie said, "He was the pawnbroker who told us about Finnbarr. He knew about Jimmy Healey's tavern, and once we got to Healey's, we found Thomas."

"And so?"

"Katherine," Annie said in amazement. "Katherine's the key."

"Good!" Charlotte said as if Annie were her prize pupil. "Keep going."

Annie took a deep breath. "Katherine knows about Mrs. Cox and Martin Belzer and their scheme, just like Timothy Dunn knew about Jimmy Healey and Finnbarr. I went through Jimmy Healey's to get to Thomas—and so I'll have to go through Katherine to get to Mrs. Fairchild."

☙

Gramercy Park was transformed. Snowdrops clustered under the trees in the little park, and shoots of yellow forsythia, bright as rays of sun, swayed against the iron fence. Annie stopped on the corner, almost afraid of her own bold plan.

Mrs. Cox bustled up the steps from the basement, market basket on her arm, exactly as Annie expected. When she had vanished around the corner, Annie crossed the street, hurried down the basement stairs and peered in the kitchen window.

Katherine was finishing the breakfast dishes. That meant Martin Belzer had left to fetch Mrs. Fairchild and Bridget at the pier. Annie opened the door and slipped into the kitchen.

"Katherine," she said.

At the sight of Annie, the color drained from Katherine's face. "Don't hit me," she said. Her hair had come loose, and it fell over her cheeks. "Don't beat me!" She put up her palms.

"Katherine, I'm not going to hit you."

"You've come to punish me, and I deserve it. I lied. I said you stole the laundry money when you never did. I'm the reason you had to leave."

"Shhh," Annie said as if soothing a frightened kitten. "We have to talk." She led Katherine up to Bridget's room, closed the door, and motioned her to sit in the rocker. Annie drew over the little stool and took Katherine's trembling hands.

"Katherine, I'm not going to hurt you. It's the truth I've come for, and it's the truth I want you to tell Mrs.

Fairchild. I didn't take anything, and Thomas didn't set any fires, but Mrs. Cox and Martin Belzer did steal all the money."

"Mrs. Cox will beat me," Katherine said. "She'll take me back to the Home for the Friendless, and she'll tell the matrons that I'm a bad girl and that she doesn't want a bad girl. And they won't want a bad girl either, so they'll turn me onto the street. I'll die on the street. I know I will." Katherine looked as if she were drowning, and Annie pulled the bigger girl to her feet, afraid to let her go on so.

"Now," Annie said, "it's not so bad as that yet. We still have time if you can tell me what Mrs. Cox is planning to do."

Katherine spoke as if from memory. "Bridget will ask for you and Thomas, and I'm to say that you're out on an errand. Mrs. Cox will insist she speak privately with Mrs. Fairchild. When they are alone, Mrs. Cox will tell her that Thomas ran away last fall and that you stole the household funds, and that she dismissed you."

"That's not fair," Annie cried.

Katherine nodded, "I know, but that's what she's going to say, and I'm to say it's all true."

"And if Mrs. Fairchild brings a Bible?"

Katherine looked away. "I'll swear on it."

"Oh, Katherine, no!"

Outside the attic window someone called, "Whoa there," and a carriage rattled to a halt.

"Quick," Annie said. "Send Bridget up and keep Mrs. Cox away from Mrs. Fairchild. Ruin the soup, break some dishes. Anything." Katherine looked horrified, but she nodded and fled, leaving Annie to pace the room and plan what she would tell Bridget.

29

"And I'll be standing right behind Mrs. Fairchild," Bridget whispered. She slipped Annie into the music room and opened the double doors to the parlor just a crack. Not for the world would Annie let Bridget go any further. Their reunion in the attic had been brief, with only enough time for Annie to tell Bridget about Thomas and Mrs. Cox and Charlotte. Bridget had rushed to alert Mrs. Fairchild and returned to say that Martin Belzer, Mrs. Cox, and Katherine had been summoned to the parlor.

Now Mrs. Fairchild, with Bridget at her side, moved slowly across the room, gathered her skirts, and settled on the sofa with a bit of a sigh. She was the same dark-haired beauty that Annie remembered from last autumn, but her trim figure was gone. Mrs. Fairchild was expecting! Annie was so pleased that she almost laughed aloud. It was only Bridget's warning glance that reminded her to stay silent. Someone rapped at the parlor door, and Mrs. Fairchild said, "Come in."

Martin Belzer and Mrs. Cox entered and arranged themselves side by side, Katherine almost hidden behind them. Martin Belzer looked larger and more florid than ever, and Mrs. Cox already had her face set in the squinched-up expression she wore when she most wanted to please.

"Afternoon, madam," Mrs. Cox said with a little curtsy.

"Madam." Martin Belzer made a bow. "At your service."

Mrs. Fairchild studied the two servants for a moment. "Mr. Belzer, Mrs. Cox, I am delighted to see you in such good health. The winter was an easy one, it seems."

And very enjoyable, Annie thought, *if you didn't mind stealing from your employers or casting children out into the street.*

"Not bad at all," Mrs. Cox said. "A bit more snow than usual, but Mr. Belzer took care of the steps and the walk." She glanced at Martin Belzer who nodded.

"Mrs. Cox, the account book, if you please," Mrs. Fairchild said and extended her hand. Mrs. Cox stepped forward, curtsied again, and handed over the gold-edged volume. Annie wondered what was recorded and what had been left out. Mrs. Fairchild leafed for a long time through the thick, cream-colored pages. At last, she closed the book and said pleasantly, "It seems that you lived a rather plain life this winter."

"Yes, madam," Mrs. Cox answered with a touch of pride. "A bowl of soup was enough on a cold day. A leg of mutton with mustard sauce and a few turnips lasted the better part of a week. 'Simple suits us best,' I've always said."

"Quite right, Mrs. Cox," Mrs. Fairchild agreed. "And Mr. Belzer, I'm impressed. The account book has only a single entry for ale and none at all for whiskey or wine. Did you take the temperance pledge?"

Martin Belzer shifted his weight and clasped his hands before him. "Ah. Yes, madam, I've changed my ways. No more drink. Only hard cider, Madam. Now and again a tumbler of hard cider."

"Admirable!" Mrs. Fairchild said. "My congratulations to you both. Would that we all practiced such modest and frugal ways. And now, Mrs. Cox, if you will hand over the remaining portion of the money I left for your expenses."

Mrs. Cox looked to Martin Belzer for help, but he just puffed out his cheeks.

"Begging your pardon, madam," Mrs. Cox said. "A terrible thing happened this winter. I hate to speak of it, I am so troubled."

"But you must," Mrs. Fairchild said and she leaned

forward and clasped her hands together. "You must feel free to tell me everything. Surely, a house with secrets cannot be a happy place for anyone, master or servant."

"No, madam." Mrs. Cox curtsied.

"Well then?"

"Perhaps just between us," Mrs. Cox said with a gesture that meant Bridget should leave.

Over her shoulder, Mrs. Fairchild said, "If you will excuse us, Bridget."

"Of course, madam," Bridget said. The next minute, Annie breathed in the scent of lavender as Bridget entered the music room. The two sisters peeked through the not-quite-shut door at the scene in the parlor.

"Now," Mrs. Fairchild said, her voice low and confidential, "tell me, Mrs. Cox, what terrible thing has happened?"

Martin Belzer cleared his throat. "Perhaps I should speak to this issue, as I am in charge of the household when Mr. Fairchild is absent." Mrs. Cox looked startled.

"It seems," Martin Belzer continued, "that the two Quinn children were not as Bridget portrayed them. We are sure it was no fault of hers, but Thomas set a number of fires in the neighborhood, and when I caught him with matches in our hayloft, he ran away. Shortly afterwards, Annie stole three of your silver spoons, and one day, when Mrs. Cox went to pay the washerwoman's daughter, the remaining household money was missing."

Annie drew in a sharp breath. Outrageous, they were! Bridget squeezed her arm to keep her quiet.

"Did you notify the police of the robbery?" Mrs. Fairchild asked. "After all, it was a considerable sum I left in your charge."

"Ah, no, madam," Martin Belzer said, and he looked down as if to study his polished boots. "I made some—um—discreet inquiries, but I didn't want to embarrass you or Mr. Fairchild by putting the family name into the police record. Still, Mrs. Cox had no choice but to fire Annie."

Mrs. Fairchild seemed to consider. "Quite so, of course. Thank you for your discretion. Naturally, this will be a terrible blow to Bridget, and I will have to speak to her myself." She paused as if thinking of the best way to present the harsh news. Her attention shifted to Katherine, and her voice grew warmer.

"Katherine, child," she said. "Step over here where I can see you." She patted the arm of the sofa. Katherine stepped closer, the wooden box of household receipts clutched to her chest. "Now Katherine, first I want to say the house looks beautiful. You took wonderful care of everything while we were gone. Thank you."

Katherine gave a little curtsy and stood up straighter.

Mrs. Fairchild said, "In addition to the housekeeping, you are in charge of the laundry, aren't you?"

Katherine nodded, and Mrs. Fairchild went on. "And, as I remember, you are very careful with all our things, writing out a list of every article that is sent out, along with notations about any spots and stains that need attention."

Katherine nodded again.

"And you give this list to the washerwoman's daughter every week?"

"I do, ma'am," Katherine agreed.

"And when she returns the clean laundry and gives you back your list, you check to see that everything has been spotlessly washed and properly ironed."

"Yes, ma'am," Katherine said, her voice growing stronger with Mrs. Fairchild's mention of her meticulous work. "After I've checked everything, Mrs. Cox signs the list and pays the washerwoman's daughter. And the girl writes 'paid in full' on the list and gives it back to me, and I put it in my receipts box." Katherine held out the box, and Annie shuddered to think that her torn and misspelled lists were still in Katherine's box.

Martin Belzer gave a little cough and let his hands fall into thick fists. "But, of course, Madam, we had little laundry this winter. So little, that I believe Katherine did it here at home. Isn't that so, Mrs. Cox?"

Annie could tell that Mrs. Cox was confused, but she

quickly collected her wits. "Yes. Yes," she said. "Of course. We sent out no laundry."

"Is that so, Katherine?" Mrs. Fairchild asked. "Do you have no receipts for laundry done this winter?"

Katherine looked down at the wooden box and cast a puzzled look at Mrs. Cox. Annie waited, sending Katherine the power to resist Mrs. Cox, willing her to tell the truth. Katherine's hands shook and the box trembled in her grasp. In a voice thin and full of sorrow, as if it had been squeezed tight and forced through a reed, Katherine said, "I did everything, Mrs. Fairchild. I did it all just as you told me to before you left. I gathered the linens, wrote the lists, and sent out the laundry, and when it came back, I checked again. It was all returned, and nothing was lost. I have the receipts." She was crying now.

"Of course, Katherine," Mrs. Fairchild stood up and put her arm around the girl. "Of course you did. You do your very best for us, and Mr. Fairchild and I notice."

Gently, Mrs. Fairchild took the box. A furrow of worry appeared between Mrs. Cox's little black eyes, and Martin Belzer stepped backward toward the door. Mrs. Fairchild opened the box and took out several sheets of paper.

"January 15, 1848," she read. "Four linen tablecloths, one with port wine stains, another with goose fat. Eight embroidered napkins, three with mint jelly, and two with egg." She switched to another sheet. "Two linen tablecloths, one stained with chocolate and another with East Indian curry." Mrs. Fairchild looked up. "Really, Mrs. Cox, chocolate and East Indian curry are hardly simple living."

Mrs. Cox pursed her lips and said, "Oh, dear, oh, dearie. There must be some mistake. Those must be someone else's table linens."

"Look for yourself, Mrs. Cox," Mrs. Fairchild said. "I believe this is your signature." She held out the lists so Mrs. Cox could examine the handwriting. "Katherine, did you shop with Mrs. Cox when she bought chocolate and curry spices and port wine and goose?"

"Yes, Mrs. Fairchild," Katherine said. "I saw her buy all those things. And Mrs. Cox and Martin Belzer, they ate on your best table linens, and they spilled things at every meal. They wrecked your beautiful embroidered cloths and napkins, and they'll never be truly clean again." Unable to hold back now, Katherine rushed on, "Annie never did take any money, ma'am. Mrs. Cox sent her away, so she could spend it on fancy recipes, and Mr. Belzer, he bought the wine to go with the food."

"Why, you little liar," Mrs. Cox said, and she stepped forward with her hand raised.

Mrs. Fairchild pulled Katherine behind her and let her sink to the sofa. She called out, "Annie, Bridget, come in please."

Annie and Bridget entered the parlor from the music room. Mrs. Cox went pale, and Martin Belzer rubbed his hands on his pants as if he were planning to fight. Mrs. Fairchild took her time.

"Annie, is Katherine telling the truth?"

"She is," Annie said. "And she tried to warn me. Katherine would have told you everything, but she is Mrs. Cox's bound girl."

Fire seemed to blaze from Mrs. Fairchild's eyes. "Monsters!" she said, spitting out the word. "That's what you are. Scoundrels, liars, thieves, corrupters of innocent children! Both of you! You are dismissed. You are never to set foot in this household again. If Mr. Fairchild or I see you on this street or even in this neighborhood, we will call the police."

Mrs. Fairchild advanced on the cook. "And you, Mrs. Cox, if you so much as write a word to Katherine or try in any other way to send her a message, I will have you thrown in jail. You will both leave immediately, and in light of your crimes, you will take nothing with you. Bridget will see you to the door."

"The recipe book," Mrs. Cox pleaded. "Just the recipe book."

"Nothing!" Mrs. Fairchild thundered.

This woman had changed over the winter, Annie

thought, and the household wasn't going to be the same. Bridget led Martin Belzer and Mrs. Cox out of the parlor.

"Katherine," Mrs. Fairchild said, helping her up from the sofa. "I apologize. If I had known your situation, I would have fired Mrs. Cox long ago. I want you to stay on with us. We'll soon have a family, and we'll need you more than ever. Tomorrow I will arrange for you to be free from all your obligations to Mrs. Cox and to anyone else. You may choose where you will go. I hope that you will stay with us."

"Oh, yes, Mrs. Fairchild," Katherine said, and Annie, without asking permission, rushed over, hugged Katherine and gave her the praise and thanks she deserved.

30

"Mam won't know me," Thomas complained. He tugged at his new jacket and poked the stiff collar of his shirt. "Can I take this off?"

Bridget brushed his hair back from his eyes and inspected the cleanliness of his ears, now visible with his new, short haircut. "Once we get to William and Ellen's,"

she said, "you can change and be comfortable again. Until then, try not to fidget."

Annie said with some satisfaction, "Mam won't know me either." She took one last look at herself in Bridget's mirror and admired the way Bridget's old suit brought out the green in her eyes and how her hair was long enough now to be pinned into a thick, shining bun. She tied on the straw hat Charlotte had helped her trim with blue ribbon and wished that Charlotte could come down to the dock with them. But Mrs. Tucker had said, "Not this time." This was a family reunion, and Charlotte would meet Annie's mother after everyone had settled in.

Annie checked the time on the watch pinned to her suit. It had been Bridget's, but now it was her own. Mrs. Fairchild had given Bridget a new watch, one on a gold chain—a present for helping to rid the family of Mrs. Cox and Martin Belzer.

"I hear Uncle Dan," Annie said. "It's time we're off."

Outside, Dan Hennessy had spruced up his wagon for the trip to South Street. He had added a bench for Mam and Bridget and draped the sides with bunting. Daisy wore wild flowers in her hat. She nuzzled Thomas's pockets for carrots while Hennessy helped Bridget and Annie into the wagon. He said, "Grand morning, ain't it?"

And it was, Annie thought. In the park, the little fountain had been turned on for the summer. Tulips filled the beds, and bumblebees droned among the blossoms on the apple trees. The whole month of May had been one glorious day after another, and now, when the city was at its most beautiful, Mam was coming.

Dan Hennessy passed the reins to Thomas, and he guided Daisy through Union Place down Broadway, Fulton, and Pearl and onto South Street. At the waterfront, the great ships with their web of ropes and furled sails made Annie thoughtful and excited.

She half-expected to see Finnbarr weave his way through the crowds. "Ireland forever!" he'd be shouting at some unsuspecting family. Dan Hennessy had seen him once, but when he'd called out a warning, Finnbarr had touched his hat and melted away.

"Stay close," Annie told Thomas. She reached for his hand but stopped herself. His time at the Five Points had taught him to take care of himself and cured him of running away. Instead he followed Dan Hennessy like a puppy, had his own newspaper corner near Jack's, and spent hours looking after Norah. In the fall, he would start school.

"Can you see Mam?" Annie asked Bridget. The *Columbia Eagle* was already tied up to a pier. Bridget shook her head.

"No, not yet."

Annie tried to remember how she had felt last summer when she had first arrived in New York. The noise and the crowd were the same, but her confusion was gone.

"Mam!" Thomas cried from his lookout atop a stack of crates. "Over here!"

Mam stood by her bundles, a lost expression on her face. She held a much bigger Dominick on one hip, and Roddy and Norah clutched at her skirts. Annie broke into a run, dodging between dazed and unsteady passengers until she nearly knocked her mother over with a wild embrace.

"Oh, Annie!" Mam said, her green eyes shining. "I'd know it was you anywhere. It's the hug to be sure."

Annie stepped back. She was as tall as Mam now, but she was strong and sturdy while her mother was bent and thin.

"Nannie!" Dominick said his old name for Annie. He stretched out his arms and buried his head in her shoulder.

Thomas shook hands with Roddy, and Bridget swung Norah up in the air, the same Norah who had been only a year old when Bridget had left. For a few moments, no one said anything. They stood in a circle on the wharf, beaming and crying, hugging each other, and marveling at their good fortune.

Annie helped Ellen put out the supper—potatoes, cabbage, milk, cheese, and bread. After much discussion, Bridget had accepted the O'Sheas offer to let Mam and the little ones board with them. Now Dominick and Roddy were finally asleep in the spare room, and Mam was resting too. The two Norahs sat under the table playing "crossing to America" with a basket of Mrs. Tucker's clothespins.

"I'd forgotten," Annie said, "how frightening everything here can seem."

"Ah," Ellen said, her brown eyes lively and her English almost fluent now. "All the church bells. Every quarter hour, it's a different peal from a different direction."

"And the cabs on Broadway. They nearly took the bunting off Uncle Dan's cart coming around Fulton."

"And the streetcar!" Ellen shook her head at the noise of the cars pulled by horses along the iron rails.

"After a while," Annie said, "Mam couldn't look. She covered her eyes and held on to Bridget."

At the mention of her name, Mam came into the living room with a burlap bag.

"Annie," she asked, "and where will you be sleeping tonight?"

Annie wished Bridget were with her, but she had gone back to help the Fairchild's new cook prepare her first dinner party. Annie said, "I'm staying at Charlotte's."

"What about the Fairchilds?" Mam asked. "I thought that once Bridget came back, you'd be back working and living there again."

"Not anymore," Annie said. She had explained to Bridget that she couldn't go back to being a useful girl. It was too confining, and Katherine was too particular. Bridget had studied her for a bit and said she thought she understood.

"The Tuckers must be generous folk to take you in like this."

"The best kind," Annie said. How could she ever explain? "But it's not all kindness. I help with the wash and repair torn lace. Mrs. Tucker pays me to keep the accounts now. I can't spell, but I can figure."

"Your father was a great one for the numbers," Mam said. "Especially the odds on the horses at the Strokestown Races." She smiled at the memory. "So you like the laundry better than fine society?"

"I do," Annie said. "Mrs. Tucker says she'll show me how to run a boardinghouse. And maybe one day we can start one."

"Ah, now," Mam said, "I've just arrived. It will be a while till I'm settled, for sure. But you'll be coming to see us, won't you?"

"You can't keep me away!"

Mam opened her bag. "I couldn't bring much," she apologized, "just a few things. This is for you."

Annie untied a bundle wrapped in a torn sheet and took out Uncle Eamon's fiddle, a match for her father's.

"I had forgotten!" she said.

"I had, too," Mam admitted. "You know how it was. Eamon's shed was so full of things, most of them half-broken. Things he was planning to patch and sell, but never got around to fixing. He could play, but it was the dancing he loved."

"He'll be wanting it," Annie said sadly.

Mam shook her head. "Eamon's been sent to Australia. In court Peter Reilly testified that Eamon was part of a gang of Irish rebels. He said they stole from wealthy farmers and plotted to kill Lord Cortland if he ever came to Ballinrea. But Hugh McDermott and the others swore that Eamon had been with them the night someone shot at Mr. Denby. In the end, the judge changed the charge from attempted murder to treason and banished Eamon for life."

Annie bent her head over the fiddle and squeezed her eyes against the tears. In their cabin, Uncle Eamon was telling stories of the fairy folk, he was leading her mother out for a reel. His blue eyes sparkling, he was doing the step dance on the pier at Galway.

Mary McDermott and her sisters, Mam and her children, Uncle Eamon, William and Ellen, the Hennessys, Jack and Norah, even Finnbarr O'Halloran and Jimmy Healey. Scattered from home they'd been. Scattered by the hunger. Scattered like notes rising from the fiddle, out over the ocean, out into the world.

From the stairwell leading to the apartment, William called, "Ellen set out all the mugs and tumblers. It's a *ceili,* a real gathering, we're having." He came bounding into the little apartment, followed by Bridget, Thomas and the Hennessys, Jack, and Norah.

Bridget rushed to hug Mam. "Are you feeling better?"

"Aye," she said. "It was the surprise of it all, so many new things at once."

Bridget touched Mam's elbow and smoothed a strand of gray hair away from her cheek. Annie counted back. It had been six years since Bridget had seen Mam. All that time, how lonely she must have been.

"Look, Annie!" Bridget cried. "Look what Mam made for me." In her hands, Bridget held a lace collar.

"It's beautiful, Mam," Annie said, admiring the tiny whorls and clusters of linen shamrocks and roses of Sharon. "When did you find time?"

"Ah, well." Mam said, "I couldn't sleep much on the boat. All the rolling and the babies crying, and the people snoring."

"And people saying their prayers in the middle of the night?"

"That too," Mam said. "And sometimes on the stormy nights, I was saying mine as well."

Bridget turned the collar over and over. "Could you make more of these?" she asked. "Mrs. Fairchild and I saw beautiful lace collars and cuffs in New Orleans. Next season they'll be all the fashion here."

Mam looked doubtful, then brighter. "It might help, wouldn't it? It'd bring in a bit for food and rent."

Bridget was excited. "I'll talk to Mrs. Fairchild. She'll know the right dressmakers." She went to show Ellen the collar.

"And Mrs. Tucker," Annie called after her, "is always needing lace mended and replaced." Annie grinned at Mam. "Ah, Mam, you're not here half a day, but your daughters have put you to work. See what Yankees we've become!" Annie stopped, her heart in her throat, her mind racing to call back the words. A traitor she was. "I didn't mean it that way. We're not Yankees, not really. We're Irish."

Mam looked at Annie and said, "Aye, you're Irish, but I can see you're also getting to be quite an American."

"But I want to stay Irish!" Annie said. "Before you came, while Bridget was away, when I was at Gramercy Park and on South Street and at the Tuckers, all I thought about was Ireland."

"For sure," Mam said, and took Annie's hand in hers, "but we don't ever stay the same, not even if we stay in the same place. You'd be changing even in Ireland. And Ireland would be changing too. So, I like my Irish-Yankee children. They take care of themselves and their mother!" She gave Annie's hand a squeeze. "Now see if that fiddle plays as well as your father's."

Annie slipped the fiddle under her chin. Almost without thinking, she tightened the pegs and plucked the strings until she found the proper tuning.

"Give us a reel," Dan Hennessy said, and he led the two Norahs out to the center of the room. With a downward stroke of the bow, Annie broke into "The Piper's Wedding." The girls circled and twirled and kicked their feet.

Jack stood up and bowed to Bridget. Annie shifted into a jig, and Thomas pulled a protesting, laughing Margaret Hennessy to her feet.

"'Star of Monaghan,'" William called and took off his coat. He ran his hands through his red hair, stepped to the center of the room, and dropped his arms at his sides. The others backed away. At the first bar of music, William leapt into the air and came down with his feet on fire. Heel, toe, inside, outside, cross in front, cross in back. In every way that two feet could move, he clicked and tapped and battered the wooden floor.

Annie played the tune at full speed, then started back to the beginning and played it again so that some notes stretched out and others broke clean. And before a single note, she put a double pat of sound, and for an old beat she tried a new rhythm. And William followed her lead, drumming his heels against her notes, talking back to her figures with patterns of his own.

On and on Annie played, and the music brought back the words to the stories she knew in her bones. And she was the warrior Fionn mac Cumhaill come to the great hall. And twenty-one Fianna gathered around twenty-one hearths in twenty-one rooms, and they dined like kings and drank from gold-rimmed cups. And after the feasting and toasts, with the blaze down to ashes, they told tales of journeys and battles, of danger and magic and courage. It had been the stories, she told herself, that carried her through. They had buoyed her spirits when she'd been alone. And for sure it would be stories that would carry her on, with family here, and home, forever, far away.

The End

About the Author

Mical Schneider is a middle-school teacher of Latin, English, and history. She lives in Washington, D.C.